Wildly

Debra Kayn

Playing for Hearts
BOOK ONE

CRIMSON
ROMANCE
F+W Media, Inc.

Published by
Crimson Romance
an imprint of F+W Media, Inc.
10151 Carver Road, Suite 200
Blue Ash, Ohio 45242

www.crimsonromance.com

ISBN 10: 1-4405-6407-8
ISBN 13: 978-1-4405-6407-9
eISBN 10: 1-4405-6408-6
eISBN 13: 978-1-4405-6408-6

Acknowledgments

To Miranda—For all your help on keeping it real, and the many times you listened as I worked out the many directions Grayson wanted to take me. What a ride! Thank you!

To Hubs—Yeah, I'm still crushin' on you, baby.

To my editor, Jess—For the wonderful work, for letting me keep my voice, and for loving *Wildly* as much as I do.

To my mom (and my dad who passed away)—Thank you for never missing a tennis match, softball game, basketball game and shelling out the money for all the tennis lessons, camps, and tournaments. Plus, the outfits, the hundreds of Nike shoes, the rackets, the strings, the cases and visors. It meant the world to me.

Chapter One

Shauna Marino walked toward the front door of Schyler Tennis Center—or straight to hell—she wouldn't know for sure until she stood before Grayson Schyler with her heart in her hand. With a toss of her hair and a fortifying breath, she forced herself to take the last remaining steps to face her past. If she'd planned the epic occasion better, she would've brought a bottle of tequila along to soften the outcome.

The wind caught the outer door and slammed it shut behind her with an ominous *whoosh*. She flinched, and then tried to hide her shaky reaction of being back in Grayson's territory by wiping the palm of her hand on the front of her white tennis skirt. She hadn't seen him in over six years, but the same anxiety-excitement-fear emotional cocktail threatened her resolve to pull this meeting off with class and calmness.

She inspected the front of her light pink, sleeveless polo shirt and flicked at an imaginary piece of lint. The odds were good that Grayson wouldn't even recognize her. Not at first, anyway.

No longer the innocent teenager, gangly and wilder than the coastal winds, always diving headfirst into whatever feelings ruled the moment, she hoped to rekindle her friendship with Grayson. Before she could show him how much she'd changed though, she'd have to prove she'd left her old ways behind her.

"Hi. Can I help you?" To the right of the door, a young man behind the front desk stood up from his perch at the computer and approached the counter.

"I have a lesson with Grayson at eleven. My name's Shauna." She stared straight ahead, her heart beating wildly in her chest.

When she'd called and made the appointment, she'd left only her first name—spelled the wrong way to be on the safe side. The idea to keep Grayson in the dark about her return had seemed brilliant at the time. She didn't want him reminded of how she'd made a complete fool of herself all through high school with her wild crush on him. She hoped the element of surprise would be enough to knock him speechless when they finally did come face to face.

Maybe then she would be able to utter the two words she should've said years ago. *I'm sorry.*

She looked up at the oversized poster of Grayson holding the Wimbledon trophy. Warmth beat out the nervousness inside her stomach, and she leaned forward. She'd never missed one of Grayson's matches on television, or an opportunity to be with him back when she'd still lived at home. It seemed like her whole life revolved around loving Grayson.

He'd started out as her idol when she was twelve years old and he was nineteen. Then, during the winters, when he came home in the off-season to teach at the tennis center, she'd used whatever creative act she could think up to spend time with him. Despite their age difference, they'd become friends. He'd fascinated her with his world travels, his responsibilities, and his goals. He was the young man who thought she was a funny kid, and she'd done whatever possible to make him laugh.

Shauna caught herself tapping the counter with her fingernail and stopped.

Looking back, she knew she'd gone overboard more often than naught, much to the disgrace of the town. But she could also point out that she and Grayson had supported each other while they'd dealt with their own individual hurts. They'd connected on a level that exceeded the normal friendships that came and went. She rubbed her arm. He'd meant everything to her. Smart, ambitious, and compassionate, he'd shown her that someone cared about her.

It wasn't until she'd turned sixteen that her world spiraled out of control, and she'd fallen head over heels in love with Grayson.

She no longer saw him as her mentor, her coach, and she couldn't accept why he'd suddenly pushed her away and left their friendship behind.

For two years, she'd gone to the extreme to reconnect with him, much to his anger. Finally, on her eighteenth birthday, she'd had enough. She was an adult, and he could no longer tell her she was a child and to stay away.

She'd shown up at his office with only her long coat covering her naked body. She swallowed at remembering how his eyes flared as she'd explained why she'd come to him. The intensity in which he'd jerked the edges of her coat closed, turned her around, and pushed her out the door devastated her.

After that, he had nothing to do with her and she'd finally accepted that she'd lost her best friend. On that horrible day when she'd decided to give everything to Grayson, her dad met her on the front porch when she'd arrived home, rejected, hurting, and broken. Grayson had ratted her out, and she was in trouble. Her stomach flipped and she inhaled deeply. Not long after, her father claimed to have had enough of her shenanigans and sent her away to college to grow up.

She'd done her best to move on with her life, and experience more of the world while attending Cal State, to forget about her past. She'd excelled in school, made friends, and a new life for herself. But, the time had come to return to where she'd grown up and repair her reputation. "Are you a registered member here?" the clerk asked.

She shook her head. "No. A guest."

At one time, she'd spent every day improving her game under the guise of being close to Grayson, but she'd dropped her membership and the sport completely when her dad surprised her and sent her to Cal State. She spun the handle of her graphite racket. Away from home, she'd waited for her feelings to change, but instead her feelings for Grayson had grown stronger.

"That'll be thirty-five dollars." The man held out his hand, and proceeded to scan her debit card before handing it back to her. "Grayson will be finishing his lesson in—" he looked up at the clock "—five minutes. Go ahead and go through the double doors behind you. You'll be playing on the clay court. If you want to warm up now, you'll be all ready when he's done. If you need anything else, my name's Daniel."

"Thank you, Daniel." She kept to the right of the counter, crossed the large lobby where onlookers gathered to observe the three indoor courts, and pushed through the double doors leading to the play area. Back to back, the grass, concrete, and clay surfaces provided every player the opportunity to practice on different playing fields.

She dawdled behind the ceiling-to-floor curtain used to block off the pathway behind the courts from flying tennis balls. She peeked between the openings of the fabric to the first court. What would one little look hurt?

Six feet away, Grayson stood with his back to her. Her stomach fluttered. All smooth, firm lines of his six-foot killer body, so close, so touchable, so out of her league. He hadn't changed a bit.

He still wore his sandy brown hair longer than most guys did, the ends only beginning to curl as they skimmed the collar of his T-shirt. His broad shoulders bunched and bulged beneath his shirt. His strong arm swung the racket in a smooth arch, showing his raw talent for the sport.

She held her breath, afraid he'd sense her behind him. Her gaze lowered to the white tennis shorts hugging his muscular ass and pulling tighter every time he moved his legs. Solid legs that left her clenching the curtain in her hand for support. Legs she would've recognized anywhere.

"Last set, Jason. Let's make each stroke count." Grayson reached into his pocket and pulled out a tennis ball, effortlessly sailing it over the net with the ease of a lifetime of practice. "Follow through…"

Shauna dropped the curtain, panting. *Oh my God. What am I doing?*

She hurried down the aisle to the appointed court and jogged out into the playing area. Keeping her back to the other players on the grass court, she raised the racket above her head with both hands and leaned to the side, stretching her back. Then she bounced on her toes and warmed up her leg muscles. At best, she hoped to muster up enough skill to play a decent game and hit the ball over the net.

If Grayson were willing to see past their history, if she could convince him she'd matured, if she proved her worth, maybe he'd believe that she'd returned a changed woman. She caught herself clutching the end of her skirt, and quickly rubbed any possible wrinkles out of the material. If she could step back into the community and erase her reputation as the wild girl of Cottage Grove, her life would finally get back on track from when she'd derailed at twelve years old.

She wasn't coming back as Tony Marino's daughter, or the child whose mother had abandoned her, or Grayson's biggest pain in the ass.

Shauna would never live down all the embarrassing things she did in the name of love as a teenager. Trailing Grayson around town, telling everyone who would listen how much she loved him, leaving him gifts, even throwing herself at him, only to be turned down cold in the end. And all through it, the whole town was laughing at her, the wild child who was obsessed with the town's golden boy.

No, she had a much more important job to do.

Two weeks ago, the city of Cottage Grove had hired her to head the Chamber of Commerce. She had plans, and if it were the last thing she tried to do, she'd impress everyone. And, maybe then, she could let go of all her guilt.

If she failed to prove she wasn't going to hurt Grayson now that she was back, then she'd have to figure out a way to move on with the black cloud hovering over her. Granted it would be with a broken heart, but she'd survive. She always did.

Out of her peripheral vision, the curtain parted. She lowered her arms and faced her lifelong love with the grace of someone who knew exactly what she wanted, terrified she'd screw up once again. *I can do this. I've changed. I'm strong. I'm mature. I'm…such a goner.*

"Shauna?" Grayson held out his hand. "I'm your instructor, Grayson."

She pried her tongue off the roof of her mouth and met his gaze while reaching for the handshake. If she accomplished anything, she hoped it was the ability to keep her game face on for the next hour. "Hello, Grayson."

Chapter Two

Shauna's sultry voice trickled over him like warm honey and his body hardened in male appreciation. How the hell could he have not met this woman before?

The corner of Shauna's mouth twitched, and the most adorable dimple showed on her right cheek. Grayson sucked in his breath, his tennis racket fell to the court, and he stepped back. *Oh, hell no.*

He squinted, trying to see the girl who'd followed him around when she was younger. The girl who had used every excuse to flirt and throw herself at him. He shook his head. No. Not possible. She wasn't supposed to come back.

The Shauna he knew wore her hair in a braid and no makeup, and always had a curious glint in her eye that left him glancing behind him for a way to escape. He studied her harder. *Jesus. Is it...?*

Her thick, wavy black hair lay wild around her shoulders, accenting the green flecks in brown eyes meant to seduce men much like a cobra ready to strike. He stared at the front of her shirt and licked his lips. The large, firm breasts she used to hide under loose T-shirts pressed against the snug fabric, and he knew without touching her the plumpness would overflow in his hands.

He leaned down and picked up his racket, taking the time to follow the length of her long legs down to the new athletic shoes. "Why are you here?"

"I haven't played for six years." She inhaled a deep breath, which had him glancing up at her chest again. "I'm ready to get back in the game..."

The rest of her words blurred in his mind, leaving him frowning. He studied the way she shrugged her shoulder and seemed almost self-conscious. Something clicked inside of him, but he had to be wrong.

He put his racket under his elbow and crossed his arms. "What are you up to?"

She paused long enough to let the question sink in, seemed to talk herself into answering, and nodded. "I have something important I'd like to talk over with you."

"Now?" He struggled to talk past the constriction in his chest.

"Another time." A smile fringed on the corner of her lips. "I paid for an hour's worth of tennis, and I mean to have you all to myself for sixty minutes."

Her admission struck a chord within him. He didn't know whether to be enthralled or frightened. Unable to deny himself the pleasure of watching her run around, he raised his brow. He wasn't going to give her an inch.

"Make that fifty minutes," he said. "The clock's ticking."

"Then we better play." She laid her racket over her shoulder, pivoted, and jogged to the other side of the court.

He watched the sway of her hips, the short ruffle of her skirt brushing her long legs, and groaned. Caught up in the past, remembering the last time he'd seen her lush body naked, he waited for her to get into position. The whole time, he wondered if she'd come back to make him pay for what he'd done.

Considering their history together, he had no idea how she was maintaining the calm demeanor. He was the mature one, the responsible one, the coach. He rotated his shoulders, hit the ball back across the net, and studied her. Her form was the last thing on his mind.

She'd changed. A lot. No longer uncoordinated, unsure, and unavailable. He ran up to the net, and smashed the ball on her side of the court. Victory was short as she ran after the ball.

It was unfair of him to take his frustration out on her. She was here for a lesson. Why?

He'd heard that from the moment she'd left Cottage Grove she'd forgotten to pick up the racket again. She'd submerged herself into school and her sorority. That was what he'd wanted for her. She wasn't like him. Tennis was in his blood, but she'd had other things that pushed her in life. At one time, he took all her attention.

She'd flattered his young ego. He'd depended on her. And when he'd realized how he was feeling toward her, he'd sent her away.

He caught the toe of his sneaker on the court. The ball sailed past him, and he clenched his teeth together. If he didn't start concentrating, she was going to kick his ass.

"Lengthen your arm. You're still holding your elbow too close to your body." He used his racket to drag a ball over to the side of his foot, and with a quick flick of his wrist, he caught the airborne ball. "Give me a forehand."

She swung, extending her arm fully. He took in the length of her limb. Long, lean, and tan. She might only be five foot six, but her legs gave the allusion of height.

"Good." He hit the ball to her.

Over and over, he drove the ball to her right side. He was an automatic machine, returning volley for volley without taking his eyes off her.

Why was she here?

No one had informed him of her coming for a visit. The last time he'd talked to her dad, he'd shared with him that Shauna was working close to where she'd gone to school. She was supposed to have a job in human resources or working in the office of some small business, and was supposed to be happy.

She did appear happy. If there was a problem with her dad, she hid it well. He gazed into her face. He used to be able to read every emotion she threw at him, but today she wasn't allowing him to see what she was thinking.

"Come up to the net." He popped a ball high, letting her run to the middle of the court.

The rosy splash on her cheeks belied her aloofness. He moved closer, hitting softer to make up for running her hard with the forehands. He narrowed his eyes. Was she smirking?

"Why are you here, Shauna?" He continued their rally.

She stretched, returned the lob. "I told you. I wanted to play."

"Tennis or with me?"

"Tennis."

He missed the ball she hit wide, and hurried to pick up a loose one next to the net. "Are you staying with your dad?"

"Yes." She twirled the racket in her hand, swaying from one foot to the other. "For now."

Unable to go on with the interrogation, he turned his back. "Take a basket of balls, and go line up and serve."

He strolled to the back of the court, and pressed his back against the curtain. Winded and sweating, he had nothing to blame it on—except the fact that she made him nervous. He needed space and time to figure out if she'd come back to pay him for what he'd done six years ago. She was never supposed to know.

Shauna jogged over in front of him, set the wire basket down, and turned her back to him. From here, he could check her out without her watching him. He zeroed in on her skirt. Damn, she'd filled out nicely. It was true. Some women were late bloomers. He'd had no idea she'd grow into her lanky body, but she did. Nicely.

She leaned over, paddled the ball three times against the clay, paused, tossed the ball up in the air, stretched—his gaze followed the length of her back—and swung. His heart pounded against his chest.

For five minutes, he tortured himself watching her serve. When there were only a few balls left, he couldn't stand it anymore. He had to touch her, to believe that she was here, that she'd come back, and that she wasn't killing him yet.

"Hang on." He walked up behind her, close enough to reach

out and sink his hands into her hair. "Line your feet up into position."

She scooted her feet apart, put her left toe behind the line, and waited. He circled his arm around her, and planted his palm in the middle of her flat stomach. The muscles in her body tensed, and he grinned behind her back. The scared little bird act brought him back to years past, when she'd try to seduce him, but the minute he'd show her any attention, she'd flutter out of his reach.

Except this time, she didn't move away. Her body slowly melted against him. He wrapped his fingers around her right hand, and slowly raised it above her head, stretching her up until she was standing on the tips of her toes. In this position, she fit into the curve of his body, and he wasn't immune. He swallowed.

"Right there." He held her in place. "When you're extending, reaching, you were bending forward. You need to keep your shoulders back, your lower back arched."

"O-okay." She shuddered.

Not letting her go, he whispered, "Tell me again why you're here."

"I got a j-job. At city hall here in Cottage Grove." Her arm shook, and he lowered his hand, not letting go of her.

"Should I be worried?"

She shook her head.

He stepped back before his reaction showed. "Continue."

Not watching, he picked up a few of the balls. A job? That meant she was back for good, or until she screwed up and got herself fired. Going by her record, that shouldn't be too long. A week, maybe, a month at most.

He jogged to the other side of the court. "Last ball. Let's play one set to finish."

The racket seemed heavy in his hand, and he leaned over into position, ready to return her serve. He chuckled to himself. This was Shauna he was worrying over unnecessarily. No matter what she tried, he'd be ready. She never got the best of him. He was always on his toes and prepared for whatever she threw at him.

Shauna took her time, tossed up the ball—keeping her back arched and knees bent the way he'd shown her—and served. The ball sailed past him. At that second, he knew he was a goner. *Score: Love, Fifteen.*

Chapter Three

"Thanks, Ella." Shauna set the phone in the cradle, and opened the bottom drawer of her desk to hide the half sandwich she hadn't had time to finish. It figured Grayson would show up early for their meeting, trying to gain the upper hand. Thank goodness her secretary had agreed to warn her of his arrival, and hadn't questioned the reason why.

She inspected the front of her white blouse. She'd give anything to appear cultured and beautiful, the way Grayson's girlfriends always appeared on television, but she couldn't do that today. Her professional attire would have to be good enough.

With one last brush down the front of her for any hidden crumbs, she scooted her chair closer to the desk and pretended to study the computer. What she wouldn't allow Grayson to see was how she practically vibrated inside knowing he would strut through the door at any second. Every day since she'd left Cottage Grove, she'd asked herself why she remained hung up on him. The answer was simple: she loved him. He'd touched her life in a way that no other person had done.

No matter how hard she'd tried to explain her unreciprocated love for him in the past, he'd brushed her off as silly. But time away never lessened her feelings, and only made her more determined to capture his heart. If he wasn't going to find her impossible to live without, she had to do something to change his mind.

That's when she'd decided to quit her job running the Women's Outreach program in Graham County and come back home.

Ella's high-pitched giggle floated past the closed door, and Shauna rolled her eyes. Even her fifty-three-year-old secretary wasn't immune to Grayson's charm. She pursed her lips and stared at the keyboard in front of her. How many times had she flirted, tried to cajole a smile, a joke, a personal reaction from Grayson, and failed? How could she compete with the other million women vying for the former Wimbledon tennis champion?

A knock startled her out of the painful memory. "Come in."

Grayson breezed into the room, nodded, and proceeded to sit on the edge of her desk instead of taking a chair the way most people would. "Okay, you've won this round, Shauna. I'm here. What's so important that we had to meet at your office, and you couldn't have talked to me after your lesson?"

She didn't need to see his onyx colored eyes to feel the fluttery sensation in the pit of her stomach. It wasn't as if she'd planned to fall helplessly in love with him. It would be much simpler if another man showed up in her life and made her heart race and her legs go weak. Maybe then she'd be able to go on with her life and be content.

"Thanks for coming by the office. I've asked you here because this is official city business." She handed him a folder, and quickly pulled back her hand. "When I took over Stan Dogger's position, he mentioned your charitable contributions toward the town in the past, and I'm hoping you'll be willing to continue that relationship working with me."

His brows lowered. "I don't see why not."

"Good. I was hoping you'd say that." She leaned back in her chair, unwilling to let his high perch on her desk unsettle her. "I want to do something big. Not only to show the city that I'm up to my new job, but also because I believe it can happen. It needs to happen."

He grunted. "I'm almost afraid to ask."

"Don't be. Together, I think we could pull off an event that'd put Cottage Grove on the map and bring some much needed revenue to a town hit hard with the closing of two manufacturing plants in the last few years." She arched her left eyebrow in challenge. "You never know, the community might be so grateful for what you can do, they'll set a bronze statue of you in the park on Main Street."

His lips twitched. "You haven't been to the park since you returned home, have you?"

"You're kidding?"

"Nope. All six glorious bronze feet of me standing in the open for everyone to look at whenever they want. The sculptor did a magnificent job matching my smile and if the rumor is true, women stand and admire my thighs before they go on their morning walk."

She rubbed her forehead. "Okay. I'm sure we can come up with something else, a day off for all city employees in your name—"

"Got it."

"How about I see if I can get you a parking spot right up front at Mr. Winston's grocery store?" She shook her head in wonder.

"Done." His smile grew. "Betty even rushes out when she sees me pull in and hand delivers one of the newer carts with well-oiled wheels."

"And you let her?" She snorted. "That's terrible."

He sobered. "You know how the town treats me."

"Still..." She pursed her lips. "You've already received the town key, right?"

He shrugged. "That lost its appeal after the third time."

"Fine. I'll have another street named after you. I noticed Main Street is now sporting a Grayson Schyler Street sign." She waited and when he seemed to think about it, she gave an unladylike snort. "The point is, what I have planned will not only benefit you, but everyone in the community...but I can't do it without your help."

"Stop for a moment." He leaned toward her and braced his hands on his knees. "You haven't changed a bit, have you? Sure, you look different, but inside you're still the same troublemaker you were back then."

No. She wasn't, dammit. She'd come back to show everyone that the Shauna Marino they'd known years ago had grown up. She wasn't going to screw up again. Grayson would see how she had learned to control her feelings and wouldn't compromise his position in the community.

This time, she couldn't fail.

"Grayson." She softened her voice. "Please, listen. This is important to me, and the town."

"Why?" he asked. "Why do you care?"

"Because I've done a lot of things I'm ashamed of, and I want to show everyone that I'm an important part of this town." She picked up the pen on her desk and clicked the end several times. "My dad did the best he could, raising me on my own, but I didn't make it easy for him after my mom left us, you know? I hurt you and everyone else I involved in my unacceptable behavior. I want to make it up to everyone."

He nodded and stood up. "What's this huge proposal you have in mind?"

She pointed at the folder in his hand. "Look at the first page and tell me about the people I have listed."

Grayson scanned the sheet, shrugged, and moved over to sit in the chair. "Bruce Coldwell's a buddy of mine. In fact, last week he returned from a Pro Bass fishing expedition in North Dakota. Gary Satchel is on hiatus until the NFL season starts. Crista Johnson—" he glanced at her, smiled, and chuckled under his breath "—I had dinner with her in Palm Springs last weekend. She's training to win the Iron Man again this year, and is in fine shape."

Shauna crossed her legs and clasped her hands together on her lap. The urge to crack her knuckles in success, get up on the desk, and dance in victory came too early. He hadn't agreed to anything, so instead she mentally clapped herself on research well done. It hadn't been easy discovering Grayson's friends. He was a private person, despite his flamboyant way of parading his string of girlfriends around in front of the camera.

"Juan Santiago is out of commission. He's recovering from surgery to repair his shoulder. I believe it was a blown rotary cup. It's iffy if he'll be ready in time for the winter Olympics. The head coach for the men's downhill ski team seems to think he'll be able to hit the slopes in time, but Juan is worried. He's young though, so he can afford to wait another four years. The last name is Dominic Chekovsky. He's at the top of his hockey career playing for the San Jose Sharks, and rarely takes time away from the ice rink. I haven't seen him for six months. The last time I talked to him, he told me he was hiding out in his home country of Russia to get away from the press here in the states." He closed the folder and leaned forward. "Now why don't you tell me what this is all about, and why you've collected a list of my closest friends?"

"I'd like to put together a charity event. I'd make simple requests on the athletes' part. It wouldn't take much of their time, but would be huge for Cottage Grove. Crista could lead a one-hour training course for kids, get them motivated about exercise, and help them realize that real people can achieve dreams. Maybe she could run a short 2k race with others if she was willing. Dominic could stand in and let people challenge him shot for shot with the hockey stick. The winner would receive one thousand dollars, which would come out of the two-dollar admittance fee." She inhaled and swallowed.

"That's all?" he huffed.

"Seriously, Grayson, it won't be hard on them. I'm only asking for three days of their time. If we could convince them to stay and eat with the community, sign autographs, even better. In return, I'll advertise the event countrywide. I project the tourism alone for the hotels, restaurants, and novelty stores in Cottage Grove will earn more than they do in a year with all the people who would come to see the celebrities."

He shook his head. "You're missing one important part of your plan that could bomb the whole idea."

"What's that?" She raised her brow.

"What's in it for the celebrities? They're taking the time and expense of coming here to help." He narrowed his eyes. "Plus, what are you willing to do for me if I help you?"

Shauna stood up and walked around to the front of her desk. "I'm hoping you could ask them, as a friend, and convince them that this would be a miracle for Cottage Grove...along with participating in the event yourself. The media attention alone will boost their career and give them extra coverage. It'll be great PR."

He sighed. "When do you want to hold the event?"

"Three months from now. The last week of September." She clasped her hands together in front of her. "The weather will be perfect, and the timing won't interfere with the kids' camp you run in August."

Grayson nodded. "Let me see what I can do. I'm not promising anything. That's a lot of different people who run on individualized schedules, and three months isn't a lot of time to rearrange their lives."

"I know, but you can do it. Everybody lov...looks up to you, respects you."

"You still haven't answered my question." He cocked his brow. "What are you going to do for me if I help you?"

She swallowed. "I suppose you won't believe me if I tell you I promise not to have a thing to do with you after we're through with the event..."

He shook his head. "You've forgotten that I know you. You never do anything without an ulterior motive. I'll need more than that."

"I-I don't have anything—"

"Oh, but I think you do." He stared at her mouth. "Sex."

"What?" She laughed to hide her gasp and the way goose bumps broke out over her body.

"I want to have sex with you." He licked his lips. "Don't tell me you're shy. You walked into my office naked when you were eighteen years old and offered yourself to me. You're no longer a little girl—" he glanced down at her breasts, "—and I want to take you up on your offer now."

Oh God. He had to bring up the one incident she'd like to forget. She smoothed her shirt over her stomach, feeling naked under his gaze. She wouldn't make the mistake of trying to seduce him again.

"That won't be happening. Remember, I'm back to help the city. Plus, I've given up on my pursuit of the great Grayson Schyler." She studied the framed picture on the wall behind Grayson. "Help me do this for Cottage Grove. The town needs help, Grayson. I've spent hours scouring through the city's accounts. Cottage Grove will be lucky to have enough money left over to pave the potholes within the city limits at the end of the fiscal year."

"I know." Grayson sighed and ran his hand across the back of his neck. "I'll see what I can do, okay?"

Shauna looked up and smiled. "Really?"

"Yeah. I'm not promising that I can get them all to agree to come and help, but I'll try." He lifted his arm and checked his watch. "I've got to go. I'm supposed to meet Stephanie for lunch, and I'm already late. I wouldn't want to disappoint her."

"Stephanie of the triple Ds and bleached hair—" She clamped her mouth shut.

She caught him staring at her, and she wrinkled her nose. Maybe she'd whispered the question, or only imagined she spoke aloud...*dammit.*

"Um...uh, that's great. Let me know as soon as you can. In the meantime, I'll work on organizing the events and I'll send you an itinerary to pass to the others. That way they'll have an idea of what will be required of them." She swallowed. The gulp seemed to echo in the silence.

"Fine." His mouth curved and he stood up from the chair, cocking his head. "I didn't know you had such a lovely impression of Stephanie."

"I don't. She means nothing to me. I couldn't care less about who you're dating." She lifted her chin and stood up straighter. "Although, Stephanie must have grandchildren by now…"

Stephanie's reputation was well known even back when Shauna was in high school. She'd often babysit Stephanie's two young children while Stephanie went out on her dates.

"Impossible. Her kids are still in school. Besides, men enjoy the company of a mature, sexually satisfying woman who knows how to—"

"Enough." Shauna stuck out her lower lip and blew the hair out of her face. *God, it's hot in here.*

"Okay." He chuckled. "I've agreed to help you. In the meantime, think about my request. I'll be in touch."

The room turned into a garbage compacter, pressing in on all sides as Grayson loomed over her. She wanted to jump up and tell him yes. Yes, she'd have sex with him, here in the office, on the floor, or every day at one o'clock if he asked.

She fought what she wanted to say, and simply said, "I'm so over you."

"Cute." Grayson chuckled as he walked away.

She watched him cross the room, her gaze sweeping over his tall frame. His broad shoulders, straight and proud, were encased in a snug, white T-shirt, and showed off a body he'd trained into shape his whole life. Graceful yet powerful, he strolled out of the room confident and secure. She sighed. Around him, she felt inadequate. She'd give anything to show him the woman she was inside, and not the awkward girl he remembered.

Chapter Four

After lunch with Stephanie, Grayson closed himself behind the doors in his office at the center. Stretched out on the lounge chair near the window, he stared up at the ceiling. In less than twenty-four hours, Shauna had wormed her way back into his life and was already messing with his head.

What should've turned into an afternoon of sex with Stephanie had fizzled the second he'd sauntered out of Shauna's office into the sunlight after their meeting. How could he throw himself into romancing Stephanie when all he saw were Shauna's flashing eyes daring him? Oh, she might not have said the words, but he saw a challenge when it came.

He never thought he'd see Shauna again, in the flesh, in Cottage Grove. When she'd left, he figured she'd go on to some big city, do wonderful things with her life, and then settle down and have a family. That's what he'd wanted for her. It was what she deserved.

What the hell was she doing back? He rubbed the spot on his chest, over his heart. She was up to something. He'd bet the tennis center on it.

He could remember exactly how he'd reacted to her yesterday in her white tennis skirt and light pink shirt, clinging to her tight but curvy figure. The buttons had been left undone on her top, leaving him glimpses of the deep valley between her breasts, and making his hands itch when she jogged back and forth returning the ball to him. She hadn't lost her skill of playing and it bothered him that his own game had spiraled out of control around her.

He'd never had trouble getting his head in the game before, but yesterday he'd fumbled with the balls, tripped over the toe of his sneakers, and one time completely missed a serve. It had taken all his concentration to keep from sporting the biggest erection in his life while on the court. At the end of the hour-long lesson, he'd been lightheaded and sweating like a pig.

What he needed to do was call up one of his standby women and lose himself in an afternoon of sex.

He enjoyed going through women the way he did tennis shoes. One-nighters, a couple hours together, a midnight rendezvous entertained and satisfied him. Long-term relationships were for other people, not him. With his kind of lifestyle, he didn't have time for love.

The Shauna that'd returned to Cottage Grove was different, but he could still see past the fake confidence. She tottered between total seductress and naïve girl next door. There was no way he could ignore the way her hands had shaken and how her breath had come in small gasps this afternoon. His whole psyche wanted to comfort her, and welcome her back with open arms. The chemistry between them had the ability to explode if he allowed it.

She'd made his life hell. As someone in the public eye, he'd gone to great strains not to allow the media to misread their relationship, which hadn't always been easy. She was stubborn, foolish, and lived in her own dreamed up world.

Still, he couldn't help appreciating her for all her eccentricity.

She'd always gone out of her way to say something nice, bake him cookies, or even sit outside on the steps at the center and babble on about the silliest thing in a time of his life when he'd needed the distraction. He'd looked forward to those times together with her, because the diversion kept him from dwelling on everything lacking in his own life.

Their friendship had seemed innocent. He was a messed up young adult, shoved into a life playing tennis with no direction off the court. Shauna had seemed to sense when he needed her the most, and he took her friendship, soaking up everything good about her to keep himself sane. With her, he could say what he wanted, laugh over her goofiness without fear of the cameras catching something on his face or in his words that he didn't want them to see.

When his parents showed no incentive to attend his matches, she'd cheered louder than anyone. He wasn't just a ranking, a bragging right, a cash machine with her. She'd honestly wanted to support him for the sole purpose of seeing him win.

After his parents died, she'd showed up more often. Most times, she'd sit with him at the center, not saying a word, silently comforting him in a way his managers and fans couldn't. With her, he had never been alone.

It was during those sweet moments with her that he'd felt normal. To everyone else, his friendship with Shauna had bordered on improper. He'd been her coach and too old to form a friendship with someone under the age of eighteen. The others in town had never understood that despite the age gap, despite the difference in their lifestyle, despite the trouble Shauna caused, they'd bonded on the most basic level. He'd needed her as much as she needed him.

She was headstrong and impulsive. He admired the way she could thumb her nose at everyone in town and dance to her own beat. Something he wanted to do many times since the age of eight, when others had already planned his life course for him. He had managers that came and went, lessons, camps, tutors who traveled the world with him, and all he'd wanted to do was shuck off all his responsibility and go fishing. He scoffed. Okay, maybe not fishing, but he definitely wanted to do whatever caught his interest at the time.

Even now, when he could do anything he wanted, he still clung to what was familiar. He was too set in his ways, and scared of forging out from under the umbrella of fame, to take another chance. When would he ever have the freedom to do what he wanted?

Going by what she'd proposed this morning, Shauna was still the same girl, only smarter. He groaned and placed his arm on his forehead. Except, Shauna wasn't an innocent anymore and he could see the advantages of working with her to help boost Cottage Grove's economy. A large part of him wanted her to pull him into whatever kind of trouble she was creating.

Was he crazy? He knew why he couldn't become involved with Shauna. It would be too irresponsible of him. He lived fast and furious. He'd only end up hurting her.

Before she'd left town, he'd been too old for her, too experienced. Now that he was thirty-one years old, he had everything: money, status, fame, and women. Relationships came and went, exactly the way he liked them.

The last thing he needed in his life was Shauna. But then why couldn't he get her out of his mind?

A soft knock jolted him out of his thoughts. He remained stretched out in the chair. "The door's unlocked."

Speak of the devil. Shauna stepped inside the opened doorway, looking tempting and fresh. "I thought I'd hand deliver the plans to you personally on my way home for the day."

She wore a tight, black skirt that skimmed the middle of her thighs. She'd swept her black hair over her left shoulder, but the strands didn't hide the way her low-cut blouse strained against her full breasts. Her chest rose and fell, and he rubbed his lips together. She'd stayed away from him for exactly three and a half hours.

"Why are you glowering at me?" Shauna raised the folder and held it protectively in front of her.

"What are you doing here?" He glanced up at her face. "Come to take me up on my offer?"

"No." She stepped over and sat the information down on his desk. "I already told you. I came to drop off the information I promised you. I finished earlier than I'd planned, and you mentioned the tight deadline, so I thought I'd jump on it. Call me efficient."

"You have a fax machine." He answered her more abrasively than necessary. "Next time, you can call my secretary and she'll give you the number, unless you want to swing by and replay the last time you knocked on my office door sans clothes."

She crossed her arms. "I'm going to ignore that comment. I assumed it would be easier to stop in and deliver them since I'm staying with my dad and I pass the tennis center on the way home, but next time I won't."

He sat up and shrugged. "Fine."

She scoffed.

"What'd you make that noise for?"

"You. I thought you forgave me for all the things I used to put you through but apparently, you're still holding it against me. I thought bigger of you." She licked her lips. "At one time, you were the only thing that kept me sane after my mom left. When I couldn't go to my dad, I threw myself into my lessons and spent every spare moment at the center. I thought we were friends. I might have been a little incorrigible—"

"A little?" He laughed. "Do you have any idea how many of my girlfriends you chased away?"

She waved off his question. "You weren't serious about any of them. Besides, I was doing you a favor."

"Some favor." He shook his head. "What about the time you packed a picnic basket and insisted I join you outside for lunch?"

"I was sixteen, Grayson." She flipped her hair over her shoulder. "All you had to do was say no."

"You asked me in the middle of a press conference!" He narrowed his eyes. "I had to go to lunch with you, or be verbally whipped every time I stepped out of the house by reporters wanting to know what was going on between us. Do you know what kind of light that would've cast over my career if they found out how you…you wanted me? I was twenty-three years old. The press would've nailed me to the billboard on the edge of town if they even thought I was returning your affection."

"I—"

"If that wasn't bad enough, you asked the camera guys to film the whole picnic. What kind of person does such a thing?" He waited for her to answer.

"Well, then, I apologize," she whispered.

"Listen, sweetheart." He stood up and stepped in front of her. "Maybe having us work together isn't such a good idea."

A gleam of deviltry flashed in her eyes. "Why? Because I drove you nuts when I was younger? How many times must I say I'm sorry…for my past?"

"You stalked me."

"Which I've apologized for many times over. Maybe you're the one having problems forgiving and forgetting." She glanced away. "Don't make me sound crazy. You were there. You felt it too."

He narrowed his eyes. "Do you still have all those pictures of me you cut out of magazines stapled above your bed?"

"No." Shauna's gaze flickered to the window, and her hesitation amused him.

"Shauna…" He leaned down, until his lips were inches from her mouth. "It'd be good between us. You're no longer a little girl, and I'm not a man who plays games. Nothing will stop me. I have no problem with taking you right here, on top of my desk, for the whole town to see. You're no longer an eighteen-year-old girl wanting to lose her virginity—there's nothing stopping me from taking what I see in your eyes."

"My eyes?"

"Mmhm." His nostrils flared. "I see how your eyelids flutter and your pupils dilate every time I step close to you."

"They do?" She raised her hand to her cheek.

"You have this little habit of catching your lower lip between your teeth, and staring at my mouth as if you want to lean forward and—"

"I do not!" She clamped her lips closed.

"Oh yeah, I'd have no problems taking what you offer me, right now." He cocked his head. "Twice."

"You would not."

"Try me."

"You seem to have a faulty memory, because I've asked you before. You chickened out. A woman doesn't forget when a man tells her no, especially when she's stripped bare, emotionally and physically." She stepped around him, but he called out her name before she could slink away. "What?"

He paused, but he never stopped looking at her. "I remember. I remember every little detail about that night. I remember how willing you were to give me your body."

"Then you walked away and called my dad."

He nodded. "Biggest mistake of my life."

"I was crushed."

"I know." He sighed. "Maybe I can make up for hurting your feelings."

"By having sex with me now?" She laughed harshly. "I don't think so."

"Do you have a ticket to McMillian's Vineyard for Saturday?"

"Grayson, don't be a jerk," she whispered. "You know how much I've always wanted to go. It's the biggest event of the summer, but my social standing in Cottage Grove hasn't changed. Heading the Chamber of Commerce isn't exactly living the high life on Knob Hill. Don't tease me."

"I never tease. That's something you should learn." He picked a ticket off the top of his desk, and handed it over to her. "Call it a welcome home gift."

"T-thank you." She stared at the white slip of paper with gold writing. "Are you going to the function?"

"I might show up." He sat down at the desk and propped his feet on the top. "It depends on if my date wants to waste her time going to a silly party instead of spending time with me…alone."

She blushed a rosy pink, which set his blood on fire. He could almost hear her thoughts, and he smirked. She wanted him, but she had no idea how to go about it. In fact, he'd bet a thousand bucks that if he put the moves on her, she'd run out the door.

"Are you taking Stephanie?" She sucked her bottom lip between her teeth.

He crossed his arms across his chest and raised his brows. He could play her game. If she wanted to pretend she didn't come back for him, he'd make her work for it. "Does the thought of me dating Stephanie bother you? This is the second time you've mentioned her."

"No!" She frowned.

"I think you protest too much." He shooed her out of the room. "You might have everyone else fooled that you're all grown up, but not me. I'm not going to protect your feelings anymore, Shauna. I want you. I've always wanted you."

"But, you—"

He held up his hand. "I only go out with women who can handle me sexually—and you want a commitment and a happily ever after. I live for the moment, because it really doesn't matter to me what happens tomorrow. If you don't want to play with fire, stay away."

Without replying, she was out the door and gone. He dropped into the chair. The hell of it was that he was fiercely attracted to her. She was a beautiful woman, but he wasn't willing to break her heart.

Chapter Five

On Friday night, it seemed as if a quarter of the population of Cottage Grove was gathered inside the Quayside Lounge. It was the first time since returning that Shauna was able to meet up with her best friends, Kate Johnson and Diana Spencer, in their old hang out. But this time, she was walking through the doors being of legal age.

Ha! Like her age had ever stopped her from wearing her sexiest blouse and top-of-the-thigh mini skirt at seventeen years old. She couldn't count the number of times she'd snuck into the lounge, acting as if she owned the place, with one purpose on her mind: to keep tabs on Grayson, and show him she was mature enough to be his girlfriend.

A shiver of nervousness skittered up her spine and she raked her teeth over her bottom lip. He'd changed in the years since she'd seen him last. He'd always been confident and sexier than any man should be allowed, but she'd noticed a new sexual prowess in him that made her nervous, excited, and every emotion in between. She hadn't been able to resist her attraction to him back then, and yesterday's meetings had proven to her that she wasn't immune to him now.

For a brief moment, she wondered if she'd get lucky tonight and Grayson would stop in at the Quayside. No, that would be bad. She had to stay strong if she was going to prove her worth to the town. Whatever happened, she was here to connect with her friends, not Grayson.

She spotted Kate, her platinum blond hair severely pulled back into a tight bun. Kate's exotic almond-shaped eyes she'd inherited from her Korean mother lit up and she waved. Shauna grinned and worked her way through the crowd. Kate grew more beautiful each time Shauna saw her.

Beside Kate, Diana lifted her glass in the air and laughed about something Kate said. Diana's short, curly hair framed a heart-shaped face that always had a hint of attitude. Shauna relaxed. Without her friends, she would have a lonely life. They accepted her and there were no judgments aimed in her direction.

Having grown up together, they had each gone their separate ways for college, but kept in continual contact and often came together whenever they could afford a weekend away to meet at the beach. Although she'd seen them last month, tonight was exciting because they were all home for good.

Kate had dropped out her sophomore year, and come back to Cottage Grove and to her boyfriend, Jackson McMillian. Diana had graduated last year and returned to Cottage Grove as the new manager at the hotel, not far from the Chamber of Commerce building where Shauna worked. Together again, Shauna truly felt at home.

Voices mingled with a Nickleback song. Laughter echoed as one rather outgoing brunette woman danced suggestively on the dance floor in the middle of the room. Shauna flipped her long hair over her shoulder and edged her way around the room.

Kate and Diana sat in the back corner of the room, by the window.

"About time you got here." Kate hugged her before scooting over and giving Shauna the closest chair to the aisle.

"Sorry." She sat and accepted the glass of wine Diana moved in front of her. "I got tied up at work, and then I needed to run back home and throw my blouse in the washer. I dropped a bite of salad on my shirt during lunch and I didn't want the stain to set in."

"What's it like being back in the house you were raised in, having your dad watch your every move?" Kate's eyes widened. "I think I'd go crazy if I moved back home. I know my sex life would suffer."

Shauna laughed. "You're such a liar. That didn't stop you from sneaking out in high school and meeting all your boyfriends down at the abandoned railroad track on the edge of town."

"True." Kate sighed. "I can't believe how long ago that was. Independence is wonderful."

"How do you like your new job?" Diana clinked her glass against Shauna's. "Isn't it wild to run into people you haven't seen in years? The talk around the hotel is you're making quite the impression. People hardly recognized you."

She laughed. "That's a good thing. I'm still ticked off at you two for not telling me how awful I looked growing up."

"Don't blame us." Kate smiled. "We knew you were gorgeous under all that hair—we didn't want you getting all the attention so we let you continue being the Jane of the group."

"Although, we had no idea your boobs would keep growing." Diana nudged Kate. "Do you think they've stopped?"

Shauna gasped. "Oh, you are not going there! I'm not the one who got the boob job the second I moved away."

Kate shrugged. "I'm proud of my yingyangs."

"Apparently, so is Jackson. He sent me a picture of them on the phone when I called to see how you were doing after surgery." Shauna grinned, and held her hands out in front of her.

"Figures." Kate rolled her eyes. "That's what I get for letting him pay for half the bill."

Diana slapped the table. "He owns one of your boobs?"

Kate widened her eyes, glancing back and forth from Diana and Kate. "Oh my God. I never thought of that. He does."

"Which one are you giving him?" Shauna raised her glass and sipped.

"Hm." Kate ducked her chin and studied her chest. "This one, I think. It's closest to my heart."

"That's exactly why I don't have a man in my life." Diana leaned back in her chair. "I'd kill myself if I acted that way."

"Jealous much?" Kate tilted her head and raised her brows.

Diana waved her question off. "Nope. I'm perfectly happy being single."

"Liar." Shauna laughed. "God, you guys. I'm so glad to be back home and have you here with me again."

The conversation continued to flow around her. She gazed out over the area, watching the people dance. For how much she expected to step back into the town she remembered, there were unfamiliar faces and a different feel to the atmosphere. Had everyone moved away or had they all changed so much, she wasn't recognizing them?

"Shauna, girl, you've got to at least look like you're up for a good time. We're back together, and we need to attract some attention. This town has turned into oldville while we were gone." Kate nodded toward Shauna's almost full glass. "What happened to all the excitement you had going for you last time we met?"

"It's probably Grayson." Diana sipped her drink. "When it comes to Shauna's happiness, it's always Grayson."

"What's that supposed to mean?" Shauna drew on the condensation gathering on the side of her glass. "I've been back a week. Even I can't get into trouble that soon. Besides, this has nothing to do with Grayson. I'm just..."

"...right back to worrying over Grayson." Diana leaned forward. "Come on, we're your best friends. Don't keep secrets from us. You're not the most patient person I know. You must have seen him already."

"I have a lot on my mind. I do have a life." She rubbed her hands together. "Lucky me received a ticket to McMillian's for tomorrow night's party. I need to buy a dress in the morning, or I'll stick out like a wannabe. For once, the stress I'm under has nothing to do with Grayson."

"What?" Diana leaned forward. "How did you get invited?"

Kate elbowed Diana. "I'm going with Jackson."

"That's a no-brainer. Jackson's a McMillian. Of course you're going, but even you couldn't sneak me a ticket. I swear you need to know a special handshake or donate a kidney to be invited." Diana narrowed her gaze on Shauna. "The question is...how did you finagle an invite?"

"Grayson." Shauna held up her finger. "No, before you ask, he didn't ask me to go with him. I couldn't get that lucky. He had an extra ticket, I guess. He doesn't even know if he's going to go... he's got a date."

"You are too good for him." Diana lifted her glass and wrinkled her nose. "What you need to do is find yourself a man that's better than him. One that's sexier, richer, and can treat you better."

With an inelegant snort, Shauna curled her lip. "There's no such man in the whole state of California better than Grayson. Everyone loves him."

Kate hissed. "I don't."

"That's because you have a boyfriend. But even you have to admit that Grayson lives up to everyone's expectations. He can't do wrong." Shauna slumped in her chair.

"Your problem is you haven't *allowed* yourself to find a better man. Trust me, there's one out there for you, you just have to recognize him. Though I still think you should come right out and tell Grayson that you never stopped loving him. Don't play games with him. Men like women who say what they want. Just go up to him and ask him if he wants to have sex. That'll get his attention, plus that's the only kind of language he'll understand." Diana pointed to an attractive man on the dance floor. "Take that guy as an example. He's good looking, moves okay, but you can tell when you get his clothes off he has some serious talent. You should practice on him."

"I'm not going to lower my standards—not for him or Grayson." Shauna leaned back in her chair. "Someday Grayson will discover that I'm not sixteen years old anymore and I'm sincere in my feelings. Right now, he can't think past all the trouble I brought him, and see me for a woman. I'm going to show him, and then you both will be eating your words."

"Grayson Schyler is too perfect, and he knows it," Diana added. "He's always been an ass to you, and in my book that wipes out all the good he does for the community. He could've at least treated you special, and not hurt your feelings."

"That's not true," Shauna said quietly. Okay, maybe it was a little true. She sighed.

Grayson's reputation as a smart businessman and a ruthless opponent on the court only touched the surface of who he really was. Deep down, he was honest, caring, and what others couldn't see but she could, was that he was a man who needed love in his life. His parents had neglected him for world travel and relaxation, leaving him alone to train and compete. Then they'd left him completely alone when they'd died on an overseas vacation.

"You need someone like Jared Studebaker." Kate gave her a cheeky grin.

She snorted. "Not on my life. The decision is still out on whether he's gay or not. He does spend a lot of time traveling to Houston, and I've never seen him with a woman. He seems to hang with his pal Irvin, from what I hear."

"He's gorgeous. His friend, I mean." Diana wiggled her brows. "Maybe I should make a play for him. I bet Irvin has a closet of clothes to die for."

"Bonus." Shauna laughed.

"The problem is we're too picky. We don't give men a chance to get to know us." Diana fished in her pocket and pulled out a twenty-dollar bill. "I think this conversation calls for another round of drinks. We all need to loosen up and have a good time. And I need to bury my jealousy about you going to the McMillian bash in alcohol."

Shauna drained her glass in two swallows. "Stay. I'll get this round. It's my turn to pay. You two bought the other drinks."

A few minutes later, she'd squeezed her way through the crowd, and found an empty bar stool. She turned around, leaned her elbows on the counter, and rubbed her temples while waiting for the bartender to make his way through the customers lined up to order.

"Shauna!" John Bigstraum leaned between her and the man sitting next to her. "I thought that was you."

She sat up straighter and smiled. "It's me."

"Your dad told me you were back." He shifted to let the man beside them leave, and then took his place at the bar. "You look wonderful. Wow."

"So do you." She patted his arm.

He really did. A few years older than herself, John had always been one of the friendliest guys in Cottage Grove. His compassion and good deeds now included training dogs for the hearing impaired and disabled. According to her dad, John's dogs were some of the best in the world.

"Congratulations on the new job. Cottage Grove is lucky to have you." John's gaze lingered on her hand. "So, catch me up on your life. You've got full time employment, you're looking beautiful…"

"Thanks." She leaned in closer. "I'm staying with my dad for the time being, but I hope to settle into my own place in the near future. Right now, I want to concentrate on my job and on getting back in the groove of living here. Sometimes it seems like nothing has changed, and then I start running into people I don't know and it feels like I've come to a brand new place."

"You'll do fine." He lifted his hand to the bartender and waved him over. "Let me buy you a drink."

"Oh…that's okay. I'm here with Diana and Kate. You remember them, right?"

"Sure I do. Talk to Diana all the time when I go in for breakfast at the hotel," he said.

"It's my turn to buy them drinks. We're starting a new tradition of girls' night out now that we're all back to living in the same town." Shauna laid her hand on his arm.

"Then let me play the hero and buy you all drinks." He winked.

"You really don't—" He placed his finger over her lips, and she laughed. "Okay, John. I'll let you buy them."

"What's your pleasure?"

"We'll have cosmos." She grinned.

"You'll have to stop by the house sometime and see the picture of Linda's kids. She's got two of them now," he said.

She scooted closer, so she didn't have to yell. "Wow. That's great. I'll do that."

His sister Linda had only been a grade younger than Shauna in school. Although they weren't close, it was a small town and they had mutual friends. She was happy to hear Linda was happy and settled.

Luke Torville smacked the palms of his hands down on the counter from the other side of the bar. "Well, well, well, look who came home. I thought I recognized that sexy walk of yours when you came in. You sure have changed."

She cringed inside while managing to offer a smile. "Hi, Luke. I didn't know you worked here now."

"I've been serving drinks here for the last four years." He leaned forward. "I think about you all the time."

She frowned. "Why?"

"Every time I drive by the school, I read 'Grayson's number one!' on the roof over the gym, and wonder what kind of trouble you're getting yourself into now." Luke laughed. "You might've been an odd little kid, but you were entertaining."

"Um. Thanks." While John ordered the drinks, Shauna took the opportunity to swivel around on the stool in hopes of ending Luke's walk down memory lane.

How long did paint last, anyway? She'd spent the whole

summer picking up litter around the soccer fields to make up for her vandalism.

John placed his hand on her arm. "The coast is clear."

She glanced over her shoulder and found Luke gone to fill drinks. "Thanks. The way people act around here makes me feel like they'll view me as a teenager forever. I'm not the same person they remember. I've lost all the angsty mood swings."

"They missed you, that's all." He cocked his head. "So, is there a boyfriend in the picture? You're dad said you weren't married."

She rubbed her arm. "Nope. It's just me."

He leaned into her personal space, and she willed herself to feel something. A flutter in her stomach, a little heart palpations, anything to signal she was a living, breathing woman. She inhaled the musky scent of his cologne in one last-ditch effort, and tried not to let her disappointment show. She felt nothing.

She studied his blue eyes, the laugh lines at the corners of his eyes, and the straight white teeth. He was handsome, young, and eager. He'd be a great catch for any woman.

"Shauna?" John brushed her hand with his fingers. "I think I lost you there for a minute. I didn't mean to pry."

She shook her head and smiled. "You're a sweet man. It's been a long day, and I was just thinking about everything I need to do yet before tomorrow's big event."

"You're going to McMillian's?" He held out one of the drinks to her, and stood up with the other two glasses.

"Yes." She inhaled deeply. "First time. I'm nervous."

"Do you have a date you're going with?"

She sipped the cosmo, swallowed, and laughed. "No. I'm going by myself. I'm still trying to convince myself that I'm really going."

"Hey, why don't we go together?" He grinned. "I got a ticket this year too, and I wasn't going to go because I didn't want to show up by myself."

"Oh...I—" She clamped her lips together. Why shouldn't she

go with John? Grayson had other plans, and probably would skip the entire event, not that it mattered. "I would love to go with you."

"Great! I'll pick you up at three." He motioned for her to lead the way back to her friends. "I'll follow you and help you carry the drinks."

She weaved her way across the room, smiling at the lucky turn of events. Tomorrow's party would be more enjoyable with someone to talk with, and John was a nice guy. *Nice guys are good.*

Chapter Six

The most sought after party of the year—hosted by Stan McMillian to celebrate the beginning of summer with a friendly fundraiser—gave Shauna the opportunity to see how the other half lived. The Grayson Schylers of the world.

She stood on the edge of the lawn beside John. Rumors of the state senator showing up, along with Cottage Grove's better-known residents, gave Shauna pause. All the schooling in the world never prepared her to talk about the stock market, oil prices, or the latest grant achieved by the hospital. She was more comfortable talking about oil changes and U-Joint replacements, thanks to her dad owning the town's only repair shop.

Attending the benefit were Peter Fontaine, a world-renowned heart surgeon, and his wife, Gloria, who headed the children's society. Next to the champagne fountain—oh lord, was that real crystal?—stood Nickolas Jenson, founder of Top Burgers, a world-famous fast food chain. She didn't recognize the blond-haired beauty beside him.

"Quite the party, huh?" John held up his glass. "Have you ever wondered how it would be to go through life having everyone cater to you? I imagine this is close to what a celebrity must feel like every day."

Shauna giggled. "I could get used to the clothes and finer things, but I'm not sure I'm up for such an active social life. You should've seen me all day. I could barely sit still, and I almost changed my mind about coming. My dress cost a hundred dollars, not a thousand. I even painted my own nails. I could never keep up with all the women here."

John slipped his arm behind her, and placed his hand at the small of her back. "I'm the lucky one to be able to claim you as my date. You look beautiful."

"Thank you." She scooted closer and leaned her head against his arm. "I'm glad you asked me to come with you. Tonight wouldn't have been the same if I didn't have someone to share the memories with or be able to whisper to when I feel out of place."

"I'm going to get another drink." He stepped away, stopped, and glanced over his shoulder. "Have you changed your mind about having a glass yet?"

She nodded, and then watched him stride away. He was attentive, polite, and made her feel like he didn't go out with women as a recreational sport. He honestly listened to her when she talked and for that alone, he made her happy.

Dressed in a navy blue suit, white shirt, and red striped tie, John looked dashing. He wasn't drool worthy the way Grayson was, but John was handsome. Everybody loved him. He had a gentle soul. Shauna liked him, and she could tell the feeling was mutual.

She walked along the grass on her toes, her heels threatening to sink into the ground. Carefully, she moved closer to the throng of people mingling in small groups dotting the area. Feeling out of place, she found it hard to enjoy the dress she'd splurged on for the event.

The black, shimmering material fell around her legs whimsically. Her shoulders and arms were bare, and she'd accented her neck with a faux diamond necklace on a thin gold chain. She'd added a touch more lipstick to her full lips and curled her hair in soft waves that trailed over her shoulders and down her back. On the outside, she appeared confident and comfortable. On the inside, she was the odd girl who more often than not had a spot of grease on her arm from her dad's shop and a pair of old cutoffs on.

"Ms. Marino, don't you look beautiful." Christine Carson, the mayor's wife and community do-gooder stepped in front of her and took both her hands. "How are you doing, dear? I've heard that you're back in town."

"I'm great." She smiled. "How are Peter and Crystal?"

"Wonderful." Christine beamed. "They entered high school this year, and Peter raves about your man, Grayson, constantly. Grayson says he has a good shot at playing at Harvard if he keeps improving."

She swallowed past the reminder that everyone knew about her love and rather immature way of showing Grayson how much he'd meant to her. "That's great. I'll have to try to come to one of his matches and watch him play."

John picked that moment to return, and she looped her arm through his. Maybe the others would recognize that she'd moved beyond Grayson, and she could put a stop to the daily reminders.

"You know John Bigstraum, don't you?" Shauna smiled.

Christine leaned forward and air kissed John's cheeks. "Of course. How nice to see you, John."

"The pleasure's mine." John handed Shauna a glass of champagne.

"Oh, look at the time." Christine placed her hand on her chest. "I should go see if Mrs. McMillian needs any help setting up for the silent auction tonight. You two enjoy yourself, and Shauna, when you see Grayson next let him know I'll be there for our meeting on Tuesday."

She shook her head. "But, I—"

Christine walked away without giving her a chance to tell her that she had nothing to do with Grayson. She sighed. *Why tell me, when she could've called Stephanie?*

The live band played and couples slowly started moving in front of the stage off to the left. Shauna sipped the drink, and wiggled her nose as the bubbles rose. She looked around for familiar faces. When she spotted Stephanie, her shoulders drooped. *Dammit.*

Stephanie was wearing a white mini strapless dress on her Barbie body, her head thrown back in laughter, and her arm swung wide, balancing a cocktail glass with a skill that impressed the handful of men circled around her. Shauna raised her glass and chugged the rest of the contents. Grayson's girlfriend of the week was everything Shauna wasn't: graceful, athletic, tall, and experienced. "At least my boobs are real."

John choked and wiped his hand across his mouth. "Excuse me?"

She groaned and curled her lip. "Did I say that out loud?"

"Yeah." He chuckled. "I'll chalk that little piece of information away, and keep it private...don't worry."

"I almost wish I could blame my loose tongue on the glass of champagne, but since this isn't the first time I've spoken my thoughts for other people to hear, I'll just pretend I didn't say anything." She studied John who continued to laugh, and slapped his arm, giggling. "It's not that funny."

"Oh yeah, it kinda is." He pulled her in front of him and wrapped his arms around her, holding her back to his chest. "That wasn't a question I had, but it's still nice to know you're one hundred percent real."

"Stop teasing me." She smiled. "What am I going to do with you, John?"

"Since you've broached the subject, I'm sure I can think of something." He leaned down and whispered, "I really like you, Shauna. I hope we can go out again."

"You know..." She leaned her head back against him. "Now that I've let my deep, dark, secret out of the bag, I might always believe you only want to date me for my boobs."

He kissed the side of her neck. "I plead the fifth."

She patted his hands clasped in front of her. "I knew you were a smart man."

Several minutes passed, and Shauna relaxed within John's embrace, swaying to the music. It surprised her how much she was enjoying his company. She was secretly glad he wanted to see her again. A distraction was exactly what she needed.

"To tell you the truth, I was always afraid of asking you out before you left town." He rubbed her arm. "I thought you had your heart set on Grayson. I'm not the only one who stayed away because of your solid stance with him."

She sighed. "It was a childhood crush, that's all. One day, I hope everyone will forget about my relentless pursuit of Grayson Schyler."

"I'm glad to hear that." John squeezed her tight. "Besides, I'm afraid Grayson is a bachelor for life. He enjoys the fast track too much, and I don't picture you as a woman who'd settle for anything less than a committed relationship."

Shauna somehow managed to hide her reaction to John's belief. Too choked with emotion from her little white lie to acknowledge his statement, she stared across the yard. John was nice, but could he ever compare to Grayson?

"Speaking of Grayson…" John muttered.

Shauna lifted her gaze and met the cold, unfeeling stare of Grayson. He stood twenty feet away with his arm around a woman she didn't recognize. She broke away from his intent gaze to check out his gorgeous date in the black and white gown that put Shauna's dress to shame.

The woman wore self-confidence while pressing herself against Grayson's side in a way that screamed of their intimate relationship. Shauna clamped her teeth together. No amount of time or training would give her that amount of sexy.

Her attention went back to Grayson. His white shirt emphasized his dark tan and the natural gold highlights in his hair. Her stomach warmed. She'd never seen him dressed with such sophistication and poise in person. Usually he ran around in shorts and a T-shirt, and while she liked him in both, the eveningwear eluded to masculine competence that left her lightheaded.

Before she could mask her displeasure at finding the cozy couple here at the party, Grayson and his date headed her way. If that wasn't bad enough, John let go of her. The loss of his body heat gave her goose bumps, or maybe it was the fact that Grayson appeared upset with her for no apparent reason, she had no time to figure out her reaction because they were suddenly standing in front of her.

"Chantel." John kissed Grayson's date's cheeks and held the woman at arm's length. "You look wonderful. When did you get back in town?"

Shauna cringed. *Great. I can't even keep my date by my side.*

Chapter Seven

"Chantel, I'd like you to meet my date, Shauna Marino." John stepped back and smiled at Shauna. "Chantel is Tom's sister. He was one of my old frat brothers, and an all-around great guy. Chantel used to come up on weekends and visit her brother at the college, that's how I met her. She models in New York now."

"It's nice to meet you," Shauna said.

Chantel's perfect, over-white teeth gleamed. "It's a delight to meet you too."

Shauna caught Grayson watching her through narrowed eyes. She smiled, letting him know she wasn't going to do anything to embarrass him. Oh sure, she wanted to ask if Chantel was his first date of the night, or if he paid her to come with him, but she wouldn't. She was going to remain polite and aloof if it killed her.

"I love this song." Chantel tugged on Grayson's hand. "Let's dance."

He shook his head. "I never dance."

Chantel's lower lip came out, but Grayson shook his head. "John, why don't you take Chantel out to the dance floor? I'm sure you guys would like to catch up on old times."

John looked to Shauna, and she nodded. "Go on. I'll be fine."

Grayson watched his date swish off and then turned to Shauna. "What are you doing here with John? I gave you one ticket." Grayson gazed out on the lawn where the others were dancing. "He's not the kind of man you need. You're high maintenance. You'll have him cowering and running for the hills before the night's over."

"You don't own me," she whispered. "I'm free to date whoever I want. I want John."

He scoffed. "Until you lose interest."

"What's that supposed to mean?"

"He'll bore you," Grayson said with a shrug, "and then you'll be back to your old self."

Shauna studied him, and ended up shaking her head. "I've changed."

"No. You haven't."

Chantel returned to Grayson's side and draped herself on his arm. "Darling? What's put that frown on your face? This is a party. You're supposed to enjoy yourself."

He smiled and kissed her lips. "I am. How could I not with the most beautiful date here."

Seconds ticked by, and Shauna smiled. "Have a good evening, Grayson…Chantel."

Shauna stepped away from him and walked over to the fountain. She held her glass under the stream of champagne and stared across the lawn. How could he flaunt Chantel in front of her? Why did he have to be so stubborn? He wouldn't even take time to get to know her again. They'd had something wonderful at one time. A friendship.

John slid his arm around her waist. "Would you like to dance?"

Would she? She blinked away the moisture in her vision and nodded. If she had to stand here and watch Grayson fawn all over his date, she was going to lose it in front of everyone.

She went into his arms and he pulled her closer, grinning. "This is nice."

"Yes." She laid her cheek on his chest and sighed, thankful for the slow dance. The hell with Grayson. She swore not to look at him again for the rest of the night.

"Are you having a good time?" John smoothed the hair down her back, lingering on her bare skin.

She nodded. "It's lovely. Everyone is so beautiful, and the night is perfect."

John swung her around, and then settled into the music. "I have to admit that when I saw Grayson, I thought you might regret coming here with me."

She pulled back and gazed up into his face. He wasn't smiling, and he appeared concerned. She inhaled a deep breath. Under normal circumstances, she would have become defensive. Everyone seemed to take a personal delight in teasing her about Grayson, but John was serious.

"Those feelings I had for him are long gone," she said quietly, her eyes downcast. They weren't, but her pride prevented her from telling the truth.

"I'm glad." He held her tighter. "I had a couple people warn me that I was setting myself up for failure by going out with you. I didn't want to believe the rumors that I didn't stand a chance."

"What have you heard about me?" She bit down on the inside of her cheek.

He shrugged. "Just tidbits about how you were infatuated with Grayson, and would plan to run into him wherever he went into town, hanging out at places he'd frequent, and flirting with him. A childish crush, I'm sure."

"That's all it was." She shook her head. "Grayson never reciprocated my feelings. Looking back, I wish I'd realized how much I bothered him, because in the end I only made myself look silly. I'm surprised anyone can see me for who I am today."

He kissed her forehead. "I don't know. I think I might like you chasing after me. What man wouldn't?"

She stood on her tiptoes, stroked his face, before giving him a soft, lingering kiss on his lips. "Thank you."

She could suddenly understand Grayson's attitude toward her. How could she have let things go so far without realizing the embarrassment she'd put him through? She'd teased and flirted, hoping to make him notice her, and all she'd accomplished was making a joke of herself.

To make matters worse, she had to deal with everyone reminding her daily of what a fool she'd been. It was humiliating to have him publicly deny her. She fought tears. The way he avoided her and always had something to say to make her feel little and immature spoke more than him coming out and speaking the truth. She clung to John and despite his company, she still came away feeling empty inside. Oh sure, she'd put on a happy face, enjoy the rest of the night, but her heart hurt.

When the crowd dispersed and everyone had headed inside, she slipped her hand into John's and followed him to the house. She handed out polite smiles to those she passed, but she couldn't shake off the feeling that her guilt followed her around in a big, black plume of smoke. She glanced behind her, and Grayson's gaze pierced her soul.

She wanted to go to him, explain again how sorry she was, but it was too late. All this time, she'd hoped he'd someday change his mind. But his expression said it all. He tolerated her, but inside he didn't feel the same.

"Shauna!" Kate reached for her and pulled her out of the crowd to the side of the room. "I caught sight of you dancing, but I didn't want to interrupt. I love your new dress. You look absolutely gorgeous."

She hugged Kate. "I am so glad to see you."

Kate held Shauna's arms and frowned. "What's wrong?"

"It's nothing important. I'll talk to you tomorrow." She glanced at John and smiled. "What do you two think my chance of winning the bid for the gorgeous diamond bracelet is?"

Kate snorted. "Considering it's under lock and key, and there's probably two security guards manning each door out of the house…none."

She snapped her fingers. "Shoot."

John laughed. "Maybe there's something more in our price range."

"I did see a gift certificate to the country club." Shauna grinned. "I'll pool my money with yours, if you want to try. It'd make a fun date in the future."

"Deal." John motioned behind him. "We better go get our seats before the action starts. Do you want to sit with us, Kate?"

"Sorry, I can't. I need to help Jackson behind the scenes. His parents have him talking business with a few of his father's business partners. You two go win." Kate leaned over to Shauna and whispered, "Another date? You go, girl."

Fifteen minutes into the silent auction, and Shauna couldn't keep up with who won what item. The men in the group ignored the silent bidding part of the rules, and egged each other on all across the room. The laughter and teasing brought out the most generous wallets, and the high priced items were quickly gone.

"Here comes the one we want." John slipped his arm behind her. "Get ready."

She pressed the paper flag she held in her hand onto his chest. "I can't do this. You do it."

He laughed. "Nope. You're going to win us our next date."

"Oh God…" She clutched the flat wooden handle tightly. "I've never done this before. I can't even understand the auctioneer when he's throwing out the price."

"There's nothing to it. When I squeeze your shoulder, lift your arm high in the air." He leaned back and crossed his legs. "You've got to be fast."

The announcement of the beginning of the bidding came and the room quieted. Shauna scooted to the edge of her chair, practically jumping up every time John gave her the signal. She forgot about the others, and put her hand on John's knee. They were in this together and it didn't matter if they won or lost, she was having a blast.

The bell rang, signaling the end of the bidding, and she collapsed back in her chair, laying her head on John's shoulder, laughing. "That was so much fun. It almost makes me wish we'd won, so we could celebrate."

"What are you talking about? You did win." John laughed and pulled her up from the chair. "We've got a prize to go collect."

Her jaw dropped, and she forced herself to recover. "What? We won? Are you sure?"

He gathered her up in his arms and hugged her. "Damn right. We've got ourselves another date and I can't wait to have you all to myself next time."

She smiled. A date. With John. Suddenly, she was looking forward to another night with him.

It wasn't until later, when they'd gone outside, that Shauna let her excitement over winning show. The beautiful evening and high spirits had her twirling around in a circle on the grass in her bare feet, shoes in one hand, the certificate in her other hand. She laughed as the cool night air washed over her. If this was the way the rich entertained themselves, then maybe she'd start playing the lottery.

"You enjoy winning." John leaned against the side of the house and watched her.

She held out her arms and danced. "Yes. It's the best thing ever. I'll remember everything about this night."

John pushed himself away from the wall, cupped her face, and gently kissed her lips. She froze, but before she could think about what he was doing, he told her to wait and he'd go round up the car. She stared out into the darkness where he'd disappeared, smiling. She could do a lot worse than John Bigstraum. He'd done everything right tonight, and she was glad she'd come with him.

"You have no idea what you're doing." A familiar masculine voice came from behind her.

She whirled around. Grayson stood over at the corner of the patio, his coat thrown over his shoulder. With all the excitement bubbling inside of her, the shadows pushing in on her, Grayson's presence was like a beacon in the night. She moved toward him, until she could see the stormy turmoil in his gaze.

"Grayson." She reached out, but he flung his coat and grabbed her upper arms, stopping her. "W-what's wrong?"

"I should be asking you that question." His eyebrow arched. "What's going on with you and Bigstraum? Are you throwing yourself at him too?"

She gasped. "Of course not. He asked me to come with him, and I'm happy I did."

"That's what you do, isn't it? You drive a man insane until he has no other choice than to take you out." He leaned in closer. "Tell me, are you going home with him? Are you going to strip out of that skimpy dress and offer your—"

"Stop!" She broke away from him. "Nothing I do is ever going to please you. What I did before...it was a mistake." She brushed the hair away from her face. "I know you don't want me. You never have. I can't compare to Stephanie...or Chantel."

She whirled around but before she could escape, Grayson grabbed her wrist. "Don't do it," he growled. "John's not the man for you."

Her legs shook, and her stomach rolled. Standing up to Grayson empowered her, yet left her weak. Why would he care what she did? She'd never gotten angry with him before, and it seemed wrong. He was the love of her life. She stared into his eyes, waiting to learn why it mattered to him what happened between her and John.

"You have no say in what I do or don't do," she whispered. "If I want to sleep with John, I will."

"Don't do it, Shauna."

She lifted her chin. "Why? You won't let yourself have me, so you don't think anyone else deserves me either. What about what I want? Don't I deserve someone who'll love me back?"

He refused to answer.

"Goodbye, Grayson," she whispered.

She slipped away and left him standing alone, his gaze burning into her back. The result of what she'd done by standing up for herself left her shivering. She'd always known somehow that he was never going to take her seriously. She was going to have to rid Grayson from her heart.

Chapter Eight

"Go, go, go!" Shauna slapped the dashboard of Diana's car and stared out the window at Grayson on the sidewalk.

He stood outside his car in front of the commerce building, his hands on his hips, glaring at Diana's small, red Honda as they left the parking lot. She sagged against the seat and latched her seatbelt. After what had happened at the McMillian party, Shauna still wasn't ready to talk to Grayson. She needed space. Of course, it didn't help that he kept showing up at her office and she kept having to find ways to avoid him. That was where Diana and her handy getaway car came in.

"Lord, Shauna, this is the second time in a row you've had me bail your ass out of trouble this week." Diana glanced over at her. "You're going to have to face him eventually. You might as well get it over with sooner than later."

"Lately, all he does is scowl at me, and I'm about to lose my composure and go off on him if he dares insult me again."

"I think the man protests too much." Diana flipped on her turn signal, and pulled out onto the main road. "You have to ask yourself why he even cares what you do."

"I was pretty bad. Do you remember that time I hid a flower everywhere he went? I even got caught skipping a day of school, so I could make it out to the center and hide them while he taught his adult classes." She stared out the window. "I've always wondered if I had something to do with his retirement."

"How could you?" Diana glanced over at her. "He wasn't even in the country when he made the announcement."

"I know, but he was only twenty-nine years old. He could've kept going. Even the press said he had a couple years left in him to hold on to the title. There were rumors that he had an injury. Some reporters even said the tennis association kicked him out for testing dirty by doing illegal drugs, which I know can't be true. Grayson refused to explain his reasons to the press, like it's some big, hidden secret. I never understood why he'd allow everyone to speculate on the reasons, and let the stories grow." She sighed. "I remember thinking it was a sign when he came back to Cottage Grove and remodeled the tennis center that he wanted me. I almost left college my senior year. God, I was so juvenile."

"Don't be so hard on yourself." Diana turned the air conditioner higher.

"The weird thing is I never did ask him why he came back or what happened to make him give up competing. It must be hard, because he's continually receiving public challenges from other players, begging him to reenter the circuit."

"Maybe your dad knows," Diana said.

"No. He doesn't. I've asked." She rubbed her forehead. "I know Grayson wouldn't tell me if I asked him now. He can barely stand to be in the same room as me."

Diana slowed down and turned into Shauna's driveway.

Shauna slipped off the seatbelt, leaned forward, and kissed Diana's cheek. "Thank you. You saved me once again."

"I'm worried about you." Diana swiveled in the seat. "I know something happened between you and Grayson at the McMillian party, but you've never so much as spoken a harsh word about Grayson before. Are you sure he didn't hurt you?"

"No." Shauna jolted when her cell phone rang. "I'm just figuring out that Grayson's not all that and decorated with glitter." She glanced at the display. "Thanks again. I need to get this. It's John."

"I'll call you later." Diana laughed. "I'll want details."

She shut the car door, waved, and pushed the call button. "John?"

"Hey, gorgeous. I've got a sack of Chinese food to go and wanted to know if you knew anyone who wanted to share my dinner with me?"

She laughed. "I might."

"What time do you get off work?" he asked.

"I just got home. Come on over."

"Sounds great. See you in fifteen minutes." He cleared his throat. "Oh, and Shauna?"

"Yeah?"

"I'm glad you said yes."

She smiled. "Me too."

It wasn't a lie. She looked forward to spending more time with John, and having him take the initiative of seeing her before their planned date next weekend made her happy. He was a considerate man, and she wanted to know him better.

She dropped the phone in her purse and headed up the path to the house. The lawn needed mowing, and the porch railing needed painting, but Shauna ignored all the things she should be helping her dad out with and headed to the garage where her dad spent most of his day, working on other people's vehicles.

The loud consuming sound of the air compressor and impact tool hid her approach. She stood beside the maroon two-door car and grinned at the legs sticking out from underneath the frame. She'd recognize those grease covered overalls anywhere.

She waited for the compressor to stop, bent down, and grabbed the hem of her dad's pants. "Watch your head."

With one pull, she rolled him out from underneath the car. He raised his brows in surprise. "What are you doing in here?"

"What? Is it a crime to visit my old man while he's working?" She planted her hands on her hips. "When are you going to sell the shop and retire to the recliner in the house?"

He growled as he pulled himself up into a sitting position. "I'm not getting older, just better looking."

She leaned down, swept off his baseball cap, and planted a kiss on his cheek before replacing his hat. "I stopped by to tell you that John Bigstraum is coming over. He's bringing me dinner. Do you want me to pop one of those potpies you love in the oven for you?"

"Nah, I'm going to stay late and get the driveline off this rig. I'll heat up a bowl of soup or something when I come in." He lay back down. "Have fun with your date."

"Hey!" She grabbed his leg, stopping him from disappearing back under the car. "Don't work too long tonight. You've been keeping late hours since I got home. You need to take better care of yourself."

He patted her cheek with his big ol' rough hand, making her feel twelve years old again. "I love you too, buddy."

Shauna left the garage smiling. Her dad was her favorite person in the world. It'd always been the two of them, even before her mom ran away from the family. There had been months prior to her mom leaving for good when she and her dad had been left on their own for dinner, her mom refusing to join them. Shauna had spent more hours than she could count lying under the car with him in the evenings, holding the flashlight or handing him tools.

Once inside the house, she straightened up the living room, carried her dad's coffee mug to the kitchen, and then took a stray pair of shoes she hadn't put away up to her room. She groaned. The pink and white bedspread on her twin bed, the stuffed animals piled in the beanbag chair in the corner, and the daisies her dad had painted in a string around her window were not a symbol of a single woman on the prowl. No way would she appear sexy and desirable with a Hello Kitty lampshade lighting the room.

"Okay, change of plans." She backed out of the room and shut the door.

She wasn't sure exactly when she'd decided to throw everything she had into building a relationship with John. It might've been between the time Grayson accused her of sleeping with John and when he'd stubbornly refused to accept her for the woman she was today. She was tired of waiting for him and, after some serious soul searching, was beginning to think that maybe she'd been wrong all these long years. Maybe it was true, and she didn't stand a chance in hell of Grayson ever loving her back.

The doorbell rang. Shauna hurried to the front of the house, and opened the door. Her smile came naturally. "Hi."

John held a brown paper sack up in front of him. "Hello back. I hope you're hungry."

"Starving." She stepped back and let him inside the house.

Dressed in faded Levi's and a buttoned chambray shirt rolled to the elbows, John appeared relaxed and happy to see her. She took the food from him and motioned him to come in the house.

She inhaled deeply on her stroll to the kitchen. "Is that chow mein I smell?"

"Yep, and I grabbed authentic wooden chopsticks." He pulled two wrapped packages out of his back pocket. "If you don't use them, I'll be disappointed."

"Oh heck yeah." She grabbed two plates from the cupboard. "Everyone knows the food tastes better when it takes all night to eat a half a cup of rice."

He laughed. "Exactly."

"Of course, we'll probably collapse from starvation before we actually succeed in eating, but it'll be good for a laugh."

"I brought extra food. I didn't know if your dad would be joining us or not." John sat down at the table.

"That was sweet of you. I stopped in the garage before I came in the house, and he said he was working late." She opened the boxes and set them in the middle of the table before sitting across from John. "I'll save him some for later. I'm sure he'll be thankful."

Shauna opened her chopsticks, and after several seconds successfully brought one small noodle to her lips. She slurped, letting the long strand slither into her mouth.

"Good?" John asked.

"Wonderful." She grinned, before setting out to capture more food. "So, how was your day?"

"Excellent." He wiped his mouth with a napkin. "Two of the dogs were placed in their new homes, and that's always a good feeling. One of them went to a young girl who's only seven…you should have seen the way she announced to her mom and dad that she didn't have to hold their hand anymore. The parents had tears in their eyes, and I believe it was the first sign of independence from their daughter that she was growing up and they could let her do things on her own. It amazes me what the dogs give back to their caregivers."

Shauna sat back in wonder. John's whole face lit up as he talked, and she could see how deeply his job affected him. Caught up in the story, she struggled with words. "That is amazing. What you do for people, through your dogs, is a miracle. You give them freedom and a new, better way to enjoy life. You're a good man, John. You should be very proud of yourself."

"It's the dogs. What I do is simple. It's the animals that rise to the occasion and show me how dedicated and special they are." He shrugged. "What about you? How do you like your new job?"

She finished chewing, swallowed, and pointed her chopsticks at him. "I'm really enjoying it. I adore educating tourists about our community, and the support from the businesses has surprised me. I'm working on a secret project right now that I'm excited about, and can't wait until everyone learns about it."

"Hm." He wiggled his brows. "A woman of mystery. I might have to see if I can convince you to share what you're doing."

She grinned and shook her head. The whole time she'd dreamed up a way to bring revenue to the town there was only one person she's wanted to share the idea with—Grayson. Now that he'd agreed to help her, she was reluctant to share their secret.

"So, have you ever been to the country club?" She leaned back in her chair and pushed her plate away.

"No, I haven't." He wiped his mouth on a paper napkin from the bag. "You'll have to direct me on what to wear. Is it suit and tie only?"

She nodded. "I think so. It'll be best if we dress up, and not take the chance of them turning us away."

They made small talk while John finished his dinner and then handed her a fortune cookie. She groaned, holding her stomach. They'd devoured the food, and she was beyond full.

"Go on. If you don't eat the cookie, the fortune won't come true." John cracked his cookie open and pulled out the tiny slip of paper. "Your days are looking brighter." He grinned. "Perfect. I've gotta believe that has to do with you. Now read yours."

As soon as Shauna opened the wrapper, the cookie crumbled all over her lap and onto the floor. She snorted. "This isn't boding well, is it?"

"Nah, that's salt. You're safe," he said.

She leaned over and picked up her fortune. "Mine says…the truth lies deep in your heart."

Horrible, soul-draining regret flooded her. Her hands shook as she brushed the pieces of cookie into her palm and stood up to dump them in the garbage. She couldn't eat another bite. Her throat had closed and her tongue stuck to the roof of her mouth. Any moment she expected a bolt of lightning to strike her dead.

She hated the way Grayson instantly entered her thoughts. He'd made it clear that she wasn't woman enough for her. Her chest tightened and she forced air into her lungs. Fear of turning into her mother almost brought her to her knees. *I am not like her. I'm not.*

What was she doing? The dinner with John was pleasant. He was attentive and smart and he had a zest for life that was apparent in everything he did.

Their conversation over dinner had been buoyant as they'd discussed their jobs, their goals, and teased each other, both skirting around the chance to grow more intimate. Still, Shauna couldn't shake the odd feeling at the pit of her stomach that something wasn't right.

The restlessness wasn't coming from John, but her. She was trying too hard to forget what she already knew. She loved Grayson.

John stifled a yawn. "Let me help you do dishes, and then I better get home. I hadn't planned to stay long, and I know we both have to work tomorrow. Is it okay if I pick you up at six o'clock on Saturday?"

"Sure. That'll give me time to do some shopping I've been putting off." She turned around and smiled. "I'm glad you came over, and I can't wait to go to the country club with you."

"Are you sure?" He set his plate on the counter, and studied her. "I'm not going too fast, am I? I'm sorta out of practice. I haven't dated much the last couple of years while I was getting my business set up."

"You're doing everything right." She patted his chest. "Don't worry about the dishes. We only dirtied two plates. I can throw them in the dishwasher myself."

She followed him to the front door and smiled when he turned around. He grabbed her hand, brought it to his lips, and kissed the back of her fingers. When she didn't protest, he pulled her close, holding her against his body. She still didn't make any move to stop him as he lowered his lips to hers for a kiss.

By the time she pushed away all her doubts and concentrated on whom she was kissing, John pulled back. Breathless and shocked over kissing someone else when her mind was on Grayson, she put her fingers to her lips. "I'll see you Saturday." John leaned over and kissed her forehead before walking down the pathway to his car.

She stood in the doorway, watching him get in the vehicle and drive away. More confused than ever, she turned to go back in the house when the loud growl of a motorcycle roared down the street. She stepped forward, excitement filling her more than any kiss. The only person she knew that drove a motorcycle was Grayson.

A young man she didn't recognize rode past the house. She sighed, disappointed. Of course it wasn't Grayson. He was probably in bed with Stephanie, not even caring if she was dating John.

Chapter Nine

The long week Shauna suffered through accounted for the two empty glasses sitting in front of her. She tapped her fingers along with the music playing at the Quayside, and smiled over the crowd, half listening to Kate describe a rather kinky night of sex with Jackson.

"…then the park ranger knocked on the window, and I thought Jackson was going to have a heart attack." Kate wiped the corner of her eye. "Of course, Jackson's body was covering me but his white ass was blocking the window."

Shauna leaned forward. "Sex in the car? How high schoolish."

"Hey, don't knock it, mean girl." Kate waved Gretchen, the waitress, over. "Another round of the same, please."

"Sure thing, girls." Gretchen eyed Shauna and crossed her arms. "You know, your message is still in the men's restroom."

"My what?" Shauna frowned.

"Call Shauna for a good time…over the second urinal." Gretchen grinned. "You should've seen all the messages that the men started writing underneath."

"Oh God." She covered her cheeks. "I forgot all about that."

"What did they write?" Kate leaned forward. "Maybe we should go in there and have us a laugh."

Gretchen shook her head. "Too late. Grayson finally noticed the message a few years ago and hired a paint crew to come in and clean it up. Although, he gave strict orders not to cover your original message. Curious, huh? I wonder why he did that?" Gretchen shook her head and walked away without waiting for an answer.

"Why would he do that?" Shauna turned to her friends. She'd snuck into the men's room, hoping Grayson would read the message but he'd left without going in there. Then she'd forgotten all about vandalizing the restroom.

Diana shrugged. "Does it matter? I thought you were all quivery for John."

"Yeah. Forget about Grayson. Let's dish John." Kate pinned Diana with a look.

"Okay, I'll ask. When are you planning on jumping in bed with John?" Diana whispered, but Shauna was sure everyone within a ten-foot radius could hear her.

"I–I don't know." She lifted her glass, remembered it was empty, and laughed self-consciously. Her vision blurred and she blinked. She probably shouldn't have skipped lunch, because she was feeling good from the drinks she'd consumed. "I'm not even sure what the rules are for this type of thing. Third date, third week…I don't even own a box of condoms."

Kate reached over and patted her hand. "You're worrying too much. John's a responsible guy. He'll have everything you need, and will make you comfortable. Although, you might not want to mention you're a virgin too far in advance. That tends to scare a guy off."

She folded her arms on the table and buried her head. "I should've lost my virginity in college with the rest of you."

"College? Try senior year of high school. That's how I kept Jackson happy," Kate said. "I think we all need another drink if we're turning this into sex talk."

"We sure do. I'm going to the bar to see what's taking so long." Diana stood up and quickly left the table.

"Listen, hon." Kate tugged Shauna's hair and waited for her to sit back up. "It's not something to be embarrassed about. You've spent the last five years finishing college and getting work experience. You're driven. Everyone who knows you understands how sweet you are. You don't fool around with people's feelings. He'll understand, and be happy to show you the ins and outs of sex. Besides, you need to get laid. You're entering nun status. I'm afraid the next thing you'll be doing is buying a cat. Don't turn into a cat woman."

"Promise me that you'll shoot me first." Shauna groaned and held up her hand. "Never mind. I'm going to pretend you didn't just say that. I'm going to keep on believing that I'm so damn sexy, some man is going to think he won the lottery when I finally spread my legs and show him what I got. Besides, I haven't been burdened in any way by not sleeping with anyone."

"Probably not, but once you start there'll be no stopping you." Kate nodded. "Sex is better than thigh-high boots."

"Mm." Shauna grinned. "Maybe we need dessert. I'm hungry, and these drinks are going to my head. I'm about ready to get up and dance."

"Lord help us." Diana returned with a tray full of drinks. "Here, drink another one before you get out there and shake your thang. You'll thank me in the morning."

Instead of removing the straw, Shauna sucked at least half the contents up and sat back, smiling. "Have I ever told you both how much I love our nights out? You're the bright spot in my life. I'm gonna be friends with you forever."

"You're dangerous when you're drunk." Kate leaned over and threw her arms around Shauna's shoulders. "If I were a lesbian, I'd take your virginity."

"I would too." Diana drew a cross in the area over her heart with her finger. "Okay, if we're all talking about some hidden sexual desire involving the opposite sex, that's a sign that we've already drank too much. We're going to have to figure out how we're getting home. I'm not driving."

"Got it covered." Kate grinned. "I already called Jackson after the last round of drinks, and he's coming to pick us up soon."

Suddenly her two friends grew silent, and Shauna glanced from one to the other, then followed their gaze to find out what had caused them to stop all conversation. Grayson filled her vision. Afraid he'd caught her frozen in shock, she raised her glass in the air.

"Hey you, just in time." She downed the rest of the drink and clunked the glass on the table. "Next round is yours."

Grayson frowned, looking at the empty glasses on the table before looking at Kate for answers. "How many of those has she consumed?"

Shauna scoffed. How typical of him to judge her. She was of legal age, and if she wanted to go out with her friends and tie one on, no one could stop her. Tomorrow was Saturday, she had a date, and not with him.

"Three." She grinned. For some reason, his anger pleased her, and made her feel vindicated. She'd show him how much she was over him.

"I'm going dancing." She stood up, swayed, and ended up grasping Grayson's arm in an attempt to keep herself standing.

"You're not a drinker." His eyebrows furrowed.

She grinned. "I wasn't until tonight, but it doesn't matter. I'm going to start living life more. I've pushed aside my interests for a long time, and now I'm going to concentrate on enjoying myself—and I'll start off by dancing."

"Shauna?"

"That's Ms. Marino to you. I'd invite you to dance, but you're…you're too cool and stuffy to be seen dancing with the town clown." She poked her finger into his bicep. "So, I'm gonna go dance, and you're gonna stay here and not dance."

Was she making sense? She shook the thought away. It didn't matter. She straightened her shoulders, stuck her chin in the air, and sauntered off.

She hadn't even made it halfway into the crowd of dancers when Grayson wrapped his arm around her waist and ushered her out the front door before she could utter a protest. The moment she caught her breath, she whirled on her heel, a little unsteady, and tried to go back in. The ground tilted and the alcohol sitting at the pit of her stomach threatened to come back up. She stilled. One hand on her stomach and the other on her forehead, she weaved as the ground tilted.

"Whoa."

Grayson came up behind her and wrapped his arms around her waist, holding her secure against his chest. "Slow down. Relax and take some deep breaths. You'll feel better in a moment."

The soft, cool breeze helped steady her. She leaned her head back and closed her eyes. In her head, Grayson had come for her. He was here, embracing her in the night. His hand stroked the bare skin of her arm. If she was dreaming, she never wanted to wake up.

"What the hell were you thinking?" he whispered, smoothing her hair off her forehead.

She twisted around in his arms and linked her hands behind his neck, plastering herself against his hard frame. She gazed up into his eyes. "I'm not thinking. I'm feeling. Admit it, you can feel this…"

"Stop it, Shauna." He rolled his shoulders and tried to move away, but she wouldn't let go.

"Kiss me, Grayson. Why are you so scared of one little kiss?" She tilted her head. "Let me prove how much I want you, how much you excite me."

"You have no idea what you're talking about. There's nothing between us. I'm thirty—"

"I know how old you are, and it only makes me want you more." She ran her finger over his lips. "You're mature, sophisticated, and sexy—everything that's made me love you over the years." She took his hand and held it above her breast. "My heart is racing because of you. No one else makes me feel alive the way you do."

"It's the alcohol talking." He stepped back, folded his arms over his broad chest, and ran his gaze up and down her body before settling on her chest. Her legs quivered. No one had ever undressed her visually the way he could, and she wanted to find out what he'd do if she took off her clothes.

She stepped forward and rose up on her toes. "Please, Grayson. Let go of the past, and see me for who I am today. I've never stopped wanting you."

In a move she never saw coming, he backed her up to the side of the building, pulled both of her hands above her head and pinned her to the brick wall. He stared down into her eyes as he rubbed his lips over her mouth. She trembled and moaned, arching her neck, reaching for him.

"What would you do if I decided to take you right here, the way you're asking me to do?" He nipped her bottom lip and she mewed. "How far will you go?"

She clutched at his shirt. "Please."

*

He sealed her lips with his mouth, deepening the kiss until she melted. Every muscle in his body tightened, and he had to hold back from being too rough. Any other woman and he would've had her skimpy skirt hiked up around her waist by now, taking everything she was offering. But this was Shauna.

She tasted sweet, intoxicating, and a little dangerous. He brought her arms down, and trailed his hands along the side of her ribs. He growled as she pressed her full breasts against his chest. His fingers burned with the heat coming off her body. She sagged against the wall, and he pressed his hardness against her stomach, keeping her standing. He couldn't seem to stop touching her.

Natural urges took over as he touched one of her round breasts for the first time. He'd spent years dreaming, imagining, fantasizing about how they'd feel. She elicited a low mewl and arched toward him, maybe urging him on, but he was too lost in the pleasure of fondling her to decipher what she was asking. He closed his hand around the curve of her breast, and his body hardened at the ripeness.

He trailed kissed down the smooth line of her neck to the open V of her blouse. His breath came hard and fast, and all thoughts escaped his thinking. No woman had ever made him lose his mind the way Shauna could.

He pulled back without letting her fall, and searched her eyes. Passion and willingness stared back at him. She trusted him. *What the hell am I doing?*

Her lips were wet and swollen from his kiss. Her heart beat wildly against him. She would've let him strip her naked, and he would've taken her in the parking lot. The raw power he received from her left him wanting to take her up on the offer, but he couldn't allow himself to use her that way. She wasn't the type of woman who'd scurry away in the middle of the night and be content with sharing a couple of hours of sex.

"Come on." He stepped back and held out his hand.

"W–where are we going?" She slipped her fingers into his palm. "Grayson?"

He kept pulling her toward his car. "Don't talk, just walk."

"Whoa…hang on there." Kate ran across the parking lot, and grabbed Shauna's other hand. "You can't just take her away without asking if she wants to go."

Grayson stared at Shauna. "Well?"

Shauna hugged Kate. "It's okay. I'll go with him."

"Sure?"

"Yes." Shauna nodded. "I'll call you tomorrow."

Kate glared at Grayson. "You hurt her again, and I'll have Jackson kill you."

He raised his brow. "I'm not going to hurt her."

"Good." Kate turned around and marched back into the lounge.

Grayson had Shauna in the passenger seat of his car, buckled in, and heading out of town in record time. He glanced at the speedometer and eased his foot off the accelerator. The sooner he delivered her home, the safer she'd be. He wanted to punch something when he thought of what could've happened to her tonight if he hadn't shown up.

He glanced beside him and softened. Typical. The first time he finally gets her alone all week, and she's too drunk to hold a conversation.

She stared out the window into the darkness. The utter silence made him feel guilty. Even though it was her damn fault. She'd forced him into the position to push her away. What was going through her head when she decided to throw herself at other men?

"If you're going to get sick let me know and I'll pull over to the side of the road." He hit the button on the door panel and cracked his window open, letting in the cool breeze, hoping to sober her up.

"I'm not going to get sick." She refused to look at him.

"It was a stupid thing you did."

"The drinking or asking you to kiss me?" She placed her head against the side window.

"Both." He shook his head. "You're old enough to realize what a dangerous situation you could have been putting yourself into by drinking and walking outside with me. If it were anyone else but me..."

"What?" She finally turned her head and gazed at him. "Are you saying I'm so desirable that any other man wouldn't have walked away when I threw myself at him?"

"Yes." He scowled. "You know damn well what I'm talking about."

"Whatever." She went back to studying the road. "Forget it ever happened. From now on, I'll limit myself to two drinks. You're safe from me. I won't be repeating that mistake again."

He pulled up in front of her house and shut off the engine. "Stay there, I'll walk you to the door."

"I don't need your help." She opened the door.

Despite how the evening was turning out, he refused to leave her outside in her condition. He followed her up to the front door, hanging back while she moved to the end of the porch and removed a key from underneath a flowerpot. She struggled with unlocking the door, and he stepped around her to do it himself, before handing her the key back.

"Where's your dad?"

She shrugged. "Probably in the garage."

He wondered if he should march across the lawn and tell Mr. Marino to take care of his daughter, but common sense told him that wouldn't be a good idea. Shauna had lived on her own for six years, and could take care of herself.

"Eat a piece of bread and drink some water before you go to sleep."

She paused with the door open, then slowly turned around. "Can I ask you something?"

Her voice came out low and husky. The anger and frustration left him. If another woman had thrown herself at him the amount of times Shauna had done, he'd tell her exactly what he thought, but this was Shauna and regardless of her insane obsession with him, he'd lived next door to her and knew her history. He'd never told her, but he admired the way she'd put her father first in her life and taken care of him. That said a lot about her, especially at her age. He also knew she put her own life on hold, and hadn't had a typical childhood without a mother in the picture. Wherever her thought process took her where he was concerned, he had no idea, but he never believed she did it to harm him.

"One question, and then you're going to bed," he said.

She stepped toward him. "Why did you leave my message on the wall in the men's restroom at the Quayside all these years?"

He turned his head and stared out into the dark. Despite knowing that every man in Cottage Grove could read the message, she'd written it for him.

"Grayson?"

His gaze went back to Shauna. Whether he could blame his need to tell her the truth on the late hour or the constant emotional battle warring inside of him since her return, he gave her his answer. "To remind myself of you when you were gone."

"Oh," she said on an exhale, her body leaning toward him.

"Go inside, Shauna," he whispered. "Lock the door."

He waited until he heard the double click, and then he cursed under his breath. Until she'd latched the door, he hadn't been sure if he was going to walk away.

Chapter Ten

"Where did the golf ball go?" Shauna lifted her hand and shielded her eyes against the outside play lights.

John pointed to the sand trap and chuckled. "Don't worry. We have a whole bucket full of balls. You'll get one on the green eventually."

She handed him the nine iron and smiled. "I'm glad you suggested coming out here after dinner. I wasn't ready for our night to end yet."

"Me neither." He swung and watched the golf ball sale through the air. "Can you imagine their electric bill? I bet it costs them quite a bundle to light up the range every night. I'm surprised we're the only ones out here. Although, I couldn't have planned it better myself."

"I'd be humiliated if anyone saw how horrible I am at golf. It's much harder than it looks." She stepped up to the tee. "This one is going in the hole. Watch."

She hooked her index finger with the pinky of her other hand, lined up her stance, took a deep breath without losing sight of the ball, and swung. John laughed, and she glanced down at the tee. The ball was still there. "Dammit."

"Here. I'll help." He guided her back into position, wrapped his arms around her, and set up her hands. "When you swing the club behind your shoulder, don't look away from the ball."

His breath brushed her cheek and she shivered. He was a good sport, and obviously had patience. She sucked at golf, but he didn't seem to mind showing her ways to improve. He trained dogs for a living, and as long as he didn't throw her a treat, she was all for learning.

"There. Don't move. Whatever you do, don't take your eyes off the ball on the tee." He moved back, letting her go. "Relax—"

"How am I supposed to do that? I'm afraid to breathe and screw up." She blew out her breath.

"Would it help to know that from back here, your stance looks great?"

She wiggled her butt. "Hey mister, you're supposed to be watching my swing."

"Oh, I am." He chuckled.

Determined to show off, she lifted the club back and swung. The twang of her club arching around her and the small vibration in the palms of her hands gave way to jubilant dancing.

"I did it!" She shimmied, holding her arms above her head.

"I knew you could do it." John swept her up in his arms and kissed her.

She froze but the longer he kissed her, she softened and gave him back everything he put into the kiss. Then, as suddenly as the kiss had begun, it was over. She moistened her lips, and a pang of regret filled her. She expected too much. After experiencing Grayson's kiss last night, how could she expect to feel the same spark, the same overwhelming sensations with John?

The lack of feelings came from her, not John. She laid her hand on his jaw and smiled. She'd love to give John everything, but Grayson owned her heart, and there wasn't enough left to give someone else. John deserved so much more.

Unwilling to let go of him, she leaned into him and sighed. "I don't think being rich is all it's made out to be. Sure, you get to dress in the latest fashion and you can do anything you want, but there are drawbacks too."

He rubbed her back. "Like what?"

"I don't know. It seems like it would be a lonely life. You could never be sure of who your friends truly are or what they thought of you. Everyone is too busy trying to climb the ladder and use each other to gain entrance into some party or business transaction. I bet none of them have ever stood out under the stars and talked about their dreams and wishes—instead they probably talk about the stock market and who was seen driving around in a new BMW."

"What kind of things do you wish for, Shauna?" John asked.

She shrugged. "Frivolous things that all normal women think about, I suppose."

"Give me the scoop. Being a man, I'm clueless about what women want."

She leaned back without letting go of him. He gazed down at her, and she could tell he was serious.

"We dream about finding someone to love us, who will never leave. It's not about finding someone who'll stick with us, but who can't live without our love. Sometimes, it seems like an impossible task," she whispered.

"You make it sound too complicated." He winked. "Men are more basic in their wants and needs."

"Maybe so." She stepped back. "It's the whole Venus and Mars thing. It keeps us guessing."

"That's true. I know you mystify me." John sighed.

"You mean, I'm unconventional." She stared out over the lawn. "I'm trying to grow up into what people expect. It seems like one week I'm making headway, and the next I do something that sets me back."

"Whoa…who says being yourself is wrong?" John leaned back and tilted her face up to look into her eyes. "You shouldn't worry about what other people think. Besides, I like you."

"Gee, thanks." She laughed and slipped out of his arms.

"No, Shauna. I mean it." He grabbed her hand and kept her near. "You're charismatic and free thinking. That's appealing."

"Yeah?" She thought it over. "I guess."

"How about I buy you a drink in the lounge before we call it a night?"

"Deal." She picked up their used clubs and put them back in the rack.

He took her arm and guided her along the path, back to the main building. Low-lying lights lit the way, and she tilted her head back and took in all the stars spackling the black sky. She stifled a yawn. Everything about tonight was perfect and yet, she felt like there should be something more. Nights were made for lovers, and John was more than attentive. She should be satisfied.

Inside the lounge, couples moved to the soft music of a live band. John led her to the bar, and ordered two glasses of wine. She shifted on her seat to look out at the dancers, her foot swinging to the music.

"Would you like to dance?" John asked.

She patted his leg. "No, that's okay. I'm kind of tired. I think the excitement of today has caught up with me."

John nodded. "It's almost midnight. You're going to have a hard time getting up for work in the morning."

"I'll live. I enjoyed myself tonight. It's worth a few hours of lost sleep."

Halfway through her wine, she yawned again. Setting the glass down, she leaned toward John. "I'm afraid the wine was a bad idea—it's relaxed me too much. I'm not trying to be rude."

"Of course not. Let's call it a night and I'll take you home."

In no time, they were in the car and on the way to Shauna's house. She reached over and held his hand. They rode in comfortable silence. Before she knew it, John had pulled up to the house, walked her to the door, and embraced her. She reached up and kissed his lips gently.

"Thank you for tonight. I had a wonderful time." She smoothed the front of his shirt. "If there's a next time, watch out. I'm going to conquer golf and surprise you."

He ran his fingers through her hair and kissed her forehead. "You did great and there definitely will be a next time. I'll call you soon, okay?"

"I'd love that." She nodded. "Good night."

"Night, Shauna." He stepped away and jogged back to his car.

With a deep sigh, she went into the house. Making sure not to make any noise, she took off her heels and tiptoed down the hall. At her bedroom, the door across the hall opened. She stopped.

"Dad?"

"Did you have a nice time?" Tony Marino rubbed the top of his balding head.

She crossed the area and kissed her dad's cheek. "Yes, I did. John's a nice man."

"He is." Tony frowned. "You okay?"

"I'm fine, just tired." She walked back to her room and paused at the door. "Good night, dad. I love you."

"Love you too, buddy." Tony disappeared back inside the master bedroom.

After taking off her makeup and slipping into an old T-shirt, Shauna climbed into bed. She closed her eyes. She really liked John, but she couldn't muster up any excitement about any future dates. She heaved a sigh. *I'm tired, that's all.*

She smiled into her pillow. Her dad was the best. How many fathers waited up for their twenty-four-year-old daughter after a date? He was the one thing keeping her from going out and purchasing her own home. Who was going to look out for him and make sure he ate and got enough rest?

Sure, he'd survived with her gone before, but he wasn't getting any younger. She flipped over onto her side and pulled the blanket up over her shoulder. He'd never dated or showed any interest in getting married again after her mom left. Belinda Marino had ruined her dad's life, and Shauna would never forgive her.

Chapter Eleven

"I've rounded up five people, besides myself, who've committed to coming to Cottage Grove during the twenty-seventh through the thirtieth of September." Grayson handed a sheet of paper over the desk to Shauna. "Two of them wanted reservations at the hotel here in town, and I've already reserved the top floor for them in my name so no one questions their arrival before you make the big announcement. It's not uncommon for me to host out of town guests at the hotel, so we're safe there. I just hope that's enough rooms for their entourage. Gary, Dominic, and Bruce will be more comfortable staying at my house."

"Great." She passed over several envelopes. "Since you're in contact with your friends, you can pass along the updated schedules and what will be asked of them down to the smallest details."

"Fine. What's next?" Grayson asked.

"I go public." She wrinkled her nose and placed her hand on her stomach. "It's make it or break it time with the business owners and the city council. I know they're going to throw all the problems this will cause within the community out in the open, but I'm prepared."

"What happens if they turn you down?"

She grinned. "I won't let them."

"Then why are you nervous?"

"Honestly?" She leaned her elbows on the desk and cradled her head. "I feel like I'm still proving myself on the job. Everyone still views me as Tony Marino's wild child. This is important to me, and I want to show everyone how I've grown up and I'm no longer the irresponsible kid who ran unsupervised in the neighborhood because her dad was too busy keeping a roof over her head."

"I think you put too much emphasis on your childhood." Grayson tapped the folder against his knee. "Your dad did his best."

"I know that, but…" She shook her head.

"But what?"

"Haven't you ever noticed how no one ever outruns their past in Cottage Grove? I imagine William Turner, the oldest living resident, is reminded daily of the time he hid the mascot at Cottage Grove High when he was sixteen. The man's almost a hundred years old, and people don't let him forget." She glanced out the window. "According to everyone, I'm still the poor girl who made a fool out of herself over a guy after her mother ran away."

The silence in the room had her wishing she could take her confession back. She rolled backward in her chair and prepared to stand when Grayson cleared his throat, stopping her.

"I don't hold that against you."

She laughed bitterly. "Oh, yes you do. How many times have you thrown my actions in my face since I've been back?"

He nodded in agreement. "I shouldn't have done that, and I apologize."

"Well…" She hid the fact she wanted to throw her arms around him in thanks. "I appreciate that, and I am sorry. If I could turn back time, I would've done things differently."

"No." His eyes softened. "To do so would've changed the woman you turned out to be."

Simple words that shouldn't have meant anything to her. But there they were, out in the open. Her breath caught and she was glad she was sitting down. It was the first sign that she was doing the right thing by coming back to Cottage Grove and putting herself back in Grayson's life.

"I—"

The intercom buzzed. "Ms. Marino?"

She held up a finger, wanting Grayson to wait while she answered the call. "Yes, Ella?"

"Everyone is gathered in the conference room, and ready for you."

"Thank you. I'll be right there." She looked to Grayson and raised her brows. "Well, this is it. Wish me luck."

He stood up as she stepped around the desk. "You won't need luck. They'll be falling over themselves wanting to help."

"I hope so." She swiftly inhaled. "I'm afraid they'll say no and I'll never find out if I can pull this off."

"Don't be. Think of them all naked, listening to every word you say." He gave her his lopsided grin.

She dropped her gaze to the front of his shorts, and squeezed her eyes shut when she realized what she'd done. He chuckled, and hooked his finger under her chin, raising her face. A shimmer coursed through her spine and she met his gaze.

"Good luck," he whispered, right before he kissed her.

He took her lips with a gentleness that surprised her, savoring, tasting, and enjoying her. Her mouth opened and jubilation swept her away. The shock value alone had her forgetting the task ahead of her, waiting in the other room. The fear of failure disappeared for that brief moment.

She let herself melt under his caress, an intimate tango between his full lips and hers. The kiss went on through her sigh and his groan. She slipped her hand under the hem of his shirt, her fingers sprawling against his skin, so hard and hot.

From out of nowhere an annoying sound persisted. A sound she knew well. *Damn, damn, damn.* She cleared her throat. "I'm coming, Ella. You can shut off the intercom."

She pulled away and rested her forehead against his chest. "I have to go."

"Mmm." He cupped her face and tilted her chin, placing one more kiss upon her lips. "Go blow them away."

She straightened her dress and smoothed her hair. She laughed, the sound more hysterical than a womanly giggle. She blew out her breath, shaking her arms and loosening the tension. *I'll show them all I can do this.*

She looked at Grayson and groaned. God, he was the best kisser.

How was she supposed to walk into the room and pretend to know what she was doing when Grayson wiped every single intelligent thought from her head? She patted her cheeks, brushed her hair behind her shoulders and stepped forward, doing her best not to look at him. She'd conquer the meeting because more than ever, she needed to prove herself.

Shauna walked down the hall with a purpose in her step, flung open the door, and smiled. "Thank you all for coming. I know this meeting was on short notice, but what I have to say will hopefully make up for the inconvenience."

She glanced from one city council member to the next, around the board table, staring back at her and expecting a miracle. Not wasting a second, she stood at the head of the table and passed a bundle of folders to Mr. Stephenson on her right.

"As you know, hard economic times have hit every person in Cottage Grove. From the outlet stores and independent bookstores, to Les's Tire Shop and Peggy Lee's Preschool. The young are growing up and instead of settling down in Cottage Grove, they're reaching out to the neighboring communities for employment. We need to create jobs and opportunities at home, before we can solve the money problems." She paused and swallowed. "To do that, we need our local companies to grow and demand in supplies to steadily climb, and we need to find a way to bring money to Cottage Grove."

"That's all common knowledge, Shauna, but times have changed. We can no more keep the young adults from moving away than we can make Cottage Grove more appealing without the funds to support a huge project." Dan Winters tossed his pen on the table and crossed his arms.

Mrs. Bakkersten clasped her hands on the table. "Dear, you've been away for a while, and we've tried everything we could think of to turn things around. Nothing has worked, and we've only dug ourselves into a deeper debt."

Shauna smiled, when what she really wanted to do was slink out of the room and forget about her whole plan. She motioned toward the folders, and then sat down.

"The documents I've handed you contain my proposal. I think all of your suggestions have been honorable and have pushed things into the right direction to bring life back into Cottage Grove, but we need something…big. Something that'll not only keep the younger generation around by creating more jobs, but that will supplement our revenue by boosting tourism." She removed a sheet of paper and held it up. "Please take a look at page three."

"What's this?" Dan frowned.

"This is a list of celebrities, well known around the world, who have volunteered to come to Cottage Grove. They've also agreed to host charity events for the locals and bring in added entertainment." She pulled out another list. "Page four consists of the activities that will be offered."

"Hold on now, missy." Mrs. Bakkersten shook her head. "Do you realize what will happen bringing in so many celebrities? Where will they stay? We don't even have enough law enforcement officers to handle extra traffic, not to mention public safety. I don't know how you can promise to have these people come when there's no money to offer them for their work."

"I understand your concerns." Shauna nodded. "Each celebrity will arrive with a full team of personnel, plus I've received a bid from a security firm to direct traffic and oversee the school and the field north of town, where the majority of events will be held. The only ones who will require a different location are Grayson Schyler, who has already agreed to account for the tennis center, and Bruce Coldwell, who will require the use of the lake for four hours. I've already talked to the county, and they've agreed to accommodate up to five hundred people without any added fees. If more show up, Bruce has agreed to stay an extra day so the crowd and safety won't be a concern."

"Humph." Mr. Stephenson pursed his lips. "What about the hotels, campgrounds, and local stores? Will they be able to keep up with the throng of people bound to come to town? What about media coverage?"

On and on, the committee asked questions, arguing their point, and each time she answered them with a growing confidence. The tension across the back of her shoulders eased, and she sat back and crossed her legs. By the time Ella came in and announced she was going home, each person had shaken Shauna's hand and congratulated her on a job well done.

They left the building with a new sense of spirit and hope for Cottage Grove. Shauna waited five minutes after the last car pulled out of the parking lot, and locked the door. Weeks of worry and stress had her wound up, and she was exhilarated. Too wired to go home, she headed out of town to Grayson's house to share the news.

Chapter Twelve

The interior beyond the locked glass doors at the tennis center lay dark. Without wondering what to do, Shauna walked around the building to the paved lane that led to Grayson's house.

Lights lined the asphalt driveway, guiding her toward the front door of the two-story colonial brick house as if they were personally urging her forward. She stepped up on the porch and rang the doorbell. A melodic chime sounded off inside.

A few seconds later, Grayson answered the door, a phone held to his ear, and motioned for her to enter. She crossed the threshold and followed him deeper into the house. That's when the magnitude of what she'd done hit her smack in the chest and left her unsure of what to do next.

She'd invaded Grayson's private domain. In all the time she'd known him, she'd never met him on his own turf. She'd respected his privacy.

"Call me tomorrow, and I'll give you my final answer." Grayson stared at her, but talked on his phone. "Okay. Talk to you then. Bye."

She bit the inside of her cheek, waiting for him to yell at her for trespassing.

"How did the meeting go?" He set the phone on the end table and motioned for her to sit down.

"Great." She remained standing. "You know, this wasn't such a brilliant idea. I didn't think my idea of coming here to see you all the way through. I'll go, and leave you alone. Maybe, you can call me tomorrow...at work, if you have time."

"Wait." He frowned. "You were all excited when I opened the door and now you look upset. What happened?"

"Nothing. I'm happy. I wanted to share with you that the committee's given me their wholehearted approval on the planned benefit. That's all. I also wanted to thank you. I think it helped, mentioning that you were helping me." She gazed around the room. "I'm sorry. I shouldn't have come here and interrupted you."

The one lamp in the room lit the area enough to see she was out of her element. This wasn't the average house with the mismatched couches and a stack of newspapers beside the recliner.

All leather furniture dotted the room, accented by red throw pillows. The floor to ceiling rock fireplace displayed two golden tennis rackets on the mantel. She squeezed the cushion of a nearby chair and sighed. Soft and plush, the leather pliable under her fingers screamed money.

"Shauna?"

"Yes?" She jerked her hands away and clasped them in front of her.

"Don't you think that good news calls for a celebration?" He cocked his eyebrow. "I was getting ready to open a bottle of wine. How about staying and having a glass with me?"

Buck up. This is my dream. I'm standing in the middle of Grayson's house, and he's inviting me to stay. "Are you reneging on your advice you gave me about not drinking? You know how I get." She lifted her shoulder and grinned. "What was it you said…I go crazy when I drink?"

"I think I can handle you." He laughed. "Besides, you deserve something nice after all the hard work you've put into the project. I don't think Cottage Grove has any idea the magnitude your idea is going to help them."

"Okay. Sure, why not. Maybe one glass." She stepped over and sat on the edge of the chair before her legs gave out. "I hope you're right. I really do want to help bring back the jobs that were lost around here. Dad's told me about some of the heartbreak, and the amount of foreclosures that've happened since the plant closed."

"It's true." He held up his hand. "Hold on. I'll go get the wine."

She barely had time to catch her breath, and he was back, handing her a full wine glass. In her hurry to calm her nerves, she almost sloshed the wine over the rim but got it to her mouth in time to save her from making a mess.

Smooth, sweet, and fruity, the wine soothed her senses and she sat back in the chair. Grayson sat on the couch and propped his feet on the coffee table. There was something extremely sexy about a guy in white sport socks.

"I take it everyone jumped on board. Did any of them give you any trouble, or did they have concerns that I could go over with them?"

She took another sip and let the liquid slide down her throat. "No. I think it went better than we both imagined it would. They had concerns, rightfully so, but I was prepared and seemed to cover all the bases."

"I knew you would do well." He smiled. "When you have a goal, you've always done everything possible to achieve it."

"Oh, Grayson, you should've been there. Everyone's attitude toward me changed. For the first time since working there, I saw hope and a new energy flowing through them all. They love this town as much as I do, and I really feel like this is going to turn things around in Cottage Grove."

He tilted his head and seemed to study her. "You love it here."

She nodded. "I always have. Even when I was younger, and complained about how everyone was set in their ways and how nothing ever changes around here. I love the small town atmosphere. Being away on my own and going to college in a big city showed me how much I missed being able to run into the grocery store and learn about my neighbors all at the same time. A five-minute trip turns into a half hour when everyone talks to you. I thought I hated that part growing up. I couldn't do anything without it getting back to my dad...or you, about what I'd done.

Granted, most of the time I was up to trouble, but it was hard."

The way Grayson watched her made her think she'd said something wrong. She drank another swallow of wine. He was making her nervous.

"You belong here," he said.

His voice was a little soft, a little rough, and caressed every nerve in her body. She shivered. There was no way she would let him know he affected her in such a way.

"This is really good." She licked her lips. "I mean, *really* good. I don't think I've had anything quite like this. It's almost got a light champagne feel to it."

He continued to stare.

Her heartbeat sped up and her nipples peaked. "What? Why are you staring at me?"

"Come upstairs with me."

She had no idea what she was supposed to say or do. In all her daydreams about the day Grayson had sex with her, she'd always willingly given herself to him. Oh sure, she wanted him in the worst way, but he only wanted one night and she'd dug herself into a hole.

There was the benefit she had to pull off, and she wasn't done making everything up to him. She gulped. And John. She couldn't forget about John.

Her hands started to shake, and she set her glass on the small table beside her chair. She looked everywhere but at him, mostly to stall. It would be so like her to blurt out, "Yes, yes, take me, I'm yours!"

He rose from the couch and kneeled in front of her chair. Cupping her face, he whispered, "I want *you*."

She pressed her cheek into his touch, melting rapidly from her core outward. "But—"

He kissed her, barely touching his mouth to hers. Her mouth trembled at the light brush of his lips. The soft, almost tender move aroused her in ways she couldn't explain. She had wanted him for so long. She couldn't wrap her thoughts around what was happening. Her breasts ached for his hands. *Do it. Tell him yes.*

"I-I can't," she whispered, against his lips.

"Yes. You can." He rubbed his cheek against the side of her face.

She shook her head and pushed him back. The moment he moved, she stood up and moved away from him. "Oh God, I'm sorry. I want you...more than you'll ever understand. But I can't."

"Why?"

She sighed and shook her head. "You're going to think I'm crazy, but we're working together on the benefit...and I'm sort of seeing someone."

He scoffed. "I'm helping you, not working for you, and John's a nobody. He's someone you're using to distract yourself from me. You're not serious about him. Two dates doesn't qualify as a relationship."

She dropped her arms to her side. "John's a nice man. He's—"

"So you're telling me no?"

"I'm sorry."

He turned his back to her and moved over to pick up his glass. He drank the remaining contents in one swallow. "Get out."

She moved forward and laid her hand on his back. "Grayson?"

"I told you before, I don't play childish games. Go home. Go back to where it's safe. Go back to John." His voice husky and deep with a passion she couldn't ignore.

She blinked away the tears and nodded. "I'm sorry."

When she reached the front door, a glass shattered in the other room, and she ran outside. She kept going until she reached her car and drove away. When she reached her house, she went upstairs and crawled into her bed, alone.

Chapter Thirteen

Grayson played to win—whether in the game of tennis or in life. And that included the women he wanted. He'd spent too many years growing up wanting what he couldn't have to waste time chasing anyone. He didn't care about the reasons for Shauna blowing him off, he was pissed.

"Damn her." He marched over and picked the phone up. He punched in numbers he knew by heart and waited.

"'ello." Bruce Coldwell's gruff voice came on the line.

"Hey. It's me. Is your cabin vacant?" He carried the phone with him as he took the stairs two at a time.

"Yeah, you need it?"

"I gotta get outta here." Grayson pulled his carryall out of the closet. "I'll have the jet take me up."

"When?"

"An hour ago." Grayson ended the call and immediately dialed Jenson, his pilot. "Gas up. We're going on a trip."

*

The next afternoon, after making the dumbest mistake of her life by running away from Grayson, Shauna walked through the front door of her house after work and found her dad embracing a woman she didn't recognize. She dropped her purse and gasped. Karma was a mean bitch.

"Daddy!" She covered her eyes and turned around.

In all the years after her father's divorce, not once had he brought a woman home. As far as she knew, he never even dated. He played poker with a few of the other men on a Saturday night once every few months, and stayed at the shop until the late hours every other day, but a sex life? No way.

"Buddy, come here."

She puffed out her cheeks, blew the air out, and slowly turned around, afraid one of them wasn't fully clothed, or God forbid, something worse. She took a few steps toward them, scanning them both in case any clothes were missing, her mind still reeling that her dad had a life outside of her and the shop.

"I've wanted to tell you since you came home, but I haven't known what to say." Tony gazed at the woman beside him and pulled her closer to him, whispering something in her ear.

Shauna looked at the woman, studying her. She appeared about her father's age, maybe older, and had short black hair spackled with gray. Her eyes were filled with pain. Shauna glanced away.

"Dad?" She went the rest of the way, and kissed her dad's cheek. "You know you can tell me anything."

"I know." He smoothed the hair off her face. "I love you so much."

Fear squeezed her heart. She grabbed his hand. "Are you okay? You're not sick?"

He smiled. "No. I'm better than I've been in a long time. I'm happy."

"Dad, that's wonderful." She squeezed his fingers.

"Buddy?" Tony moved behind her and held on to her shoulders, turning her until she was in front of the woman. "I know it's been a long time, but look hard."

The woman's chin quivered and her green eyes shone back brightly, as if holding back tears. Shauna frowned. The woman looked like...*oh God. No. No. No.*

There were wrinkles around her eyes, but the pencil thin eyebrows and the familiarity in the woman's gaze stared back at her. She covered her mouth and shook her head in denial.

"Hi, honey." Belinda Marino reached for her with a shaky hand.

Shauna jerked back before her mother could touch her, and turned toward her dad. "Don't tell me you let her come back. She left us twelve years ago."

"Shauna!" He grabbed her arm. "She's your mother. I didn't teach you to be rude."

She pulled out of his grasp. "Is s-she staying here?"

Tony nodded. "Yes. She's been staying at the hotel since you came home. She wanted you to get used to having her back before we told you we're living together. If you want to blame someone, I'll be the one responsible for not telling you sooner. I wanted you to get used to living here again before I sprang this on you."

She blinked. Hard.

"Shauna, please…" Tony whispered.

"No." She backed up. "I gotta go. If she's staying in this house, I can't stay here."

She turned and headed upstairs. *This isn't happening.*

How dare her mother come here after what she did to the family. To her dad. To her. She wasn't wanted. Belinda had torn them apart and taken Shauna's whole childhood away when she'd left the house in the middle of the night. What kind of mother does that to their child?

She stuffed her work clothes in a suitcase and grabbed her makeup bag and a few pairs of shoes. Without stopping to think of where she was going or what she was going to do, she walked down the stairs.

"Don't go, buddy. Let's sleep on it. We'll talk tomorrow." Tony blocked the door.

She stood on tiptoe and kissed her dad's cheek. "I can't."

"Where will you go?"

"Don't worry." She squared her shoulders. "I've been on my own for the last six years. I'll find somewhere to stay."

"I love you." Tony stepped out of her way. "I love your mom too."

Shauna never looked behind her, but opened the door and carried her things to the car. Numb and shocked, she slid into the driver's seat and drove away.

For reasons Shauna had never learned, Belinda had disappeared from the house while Shauna had gone to school. No note, no goodbye, no kiss. She'd simply exited their lives without a scene.

Except she'd left behind a lot of damage. All these years, Shauna had thought the reason her dad worked long hours was to distract himself from the truth. Belinda never loved them, only herself. But that wasn't true anymore. She'd obviously come back and made things right with Tony when Shauna was in college. Why hadn't he told her?

Shauna turned into the entrance of the tennis center, automatically running to the one person who'd been there for her after her mom had abandoned her the first time.

Grayson had no idea how much his continual presence in her life meant to her. When she was younger, the one constant person in her life had been Grayson. Every day at three o'clock, she'd enter the center, take a lesson, and hang out there with the other kids, often talking to Grayson or watching him teach another class until it was dinnertime and she walked home to her dad.

She parked the car and knocked on the front door. Her head hurt, but the numbness over the shock of learning her mother was in Cottage Grove wouldn't let her dwell on the pain. *Please, open up.*

She rapped on the door again.

Seconds ticked by and still Grayson hadn't opened the door. She peered up at the windows. They were all dark.

Heaviness settled over her, and she swallowed the lump that rose in her chest and threatened to bring her to her knees. She walked back to her car. For the first time tonight, a tear wet her cheek. Then another one followed.

Chapter Fourteen

The rumble of a truck coming up the gravel road broke the silence in the Gifford forest. Grayson remained sitting in the rocker on the porch of Bruce's cabin. Out here, away from society, the visitor could only be one person.

A few minutes later, Bruce Coldwell lumbered out of the pumped up four-wheeler and headed toward Grayson. Lean and tan, Bruce spent the majority of his time outdoors near water. The world champion bass fisherman led a life of luxury and owned homes on more waterways than he could count, including the quaint four-bedroom cabin Grayson sometimes borrowed to get away from it all.

This morning Bruce wore his sun-bleached hair loose around his shoulders, and by the looks of it, hadn't shaved for a couple weeks. Grayson lifted his chin in greeting.

"You're a sight for sore eyes." Bruce held out his hand and shook Grayson's. "I thought I'd drive up and see what's going on."

"'Bout an hour ago a doe walked to the edge of the water, drank, and went back into the woods." Grayson folded his arms across his chest.

Bruce sat down on the empty chair. "Well, that'll make the newspapers, I'm sure. Are you positive you didn't see any bears or maybe a pack of wolves? That seems to create more of a buzz."

"Nope." Grayson sighed and set motion to his rocker.

He'd sat outside all night, trying to find the calm inside of him. Solitude always helped him gather his thoughts and focus his energy. He didn't get to be a Wimbledon champion by losing his temper or letting the outside world faze him. Unfortunately, dealing with Shauna was harder than playing tennis, and he still hadn't come up with a solution to his problem.

"Wanna talk about what's going on with you? You haven't come up here to get away from life for at least a year." Bruce stretched his legs out and crossed his ankles before latching his hands together behind his head.

"Not really," he said.

Grayson wanted to stand up and throw Bruce and the damn chair off the porch. There was nothing anyone could do to help him make any of this better. He would have to figure out how to climb out of the shithole he dug himself. The way his life was going, it probably wasn't going to be any time soon if Shauna stuck around.

He hadn't relaxed since Shauna strolled back into town and pretended not to have any feelings for him. Oh, she tried to fool him, but she couldn't hide her true feelings from him. Every emotion played across her face, and he knew them all. She might've come back more mature and educated, but there was no denying the way her eyes still shone when she looked at him.

What he couldn't understand was why she'd turned him down. They were adults. Adults had sex. It didn't have to change anything between them. Hell, he didn't want it to change. He liked the single life, and not answering to anyone else. He'd worked damn hard to gain his freedom, and he wasn't going to ruin it.

"Grayson...I'm your friend. If something is going on, I want to help you. You'd do the same thing for me, wouldn't you?"

"Yeah, you know I would." He ran his hands over his face. "My problem isn't simple."

"Hell, we've been through a lot together. It can't be that bad." Bruce turned. "Is it woman trouble?"

He nodded. "She's a pain in my ass."

"Yeah?" Bruce chuckled. "Aren't they all?"

"I never have problems getting a woman in bed." He snorted. "There are times I can't keep them out. This one...she's different."

"Turned you down, huh?"

"Shot me in the chest before I could even talk her into it. All I could think about was getting the hell out of town." He shook his head. "The damn thing is I shouldn't even like her. I've known her forever. She's a friend who helped me survive growing up in Cottage Grove. She kept me sane." He snorted. "I swear she's out to cause me nothing but misery. Do you know she has it in her head that she loves me? She's more persistent than any opponent I've faced on the courts."

"Jesus, Gray…" Bruce slapped him on the shoulder. "Are you talking about that young chick that used to stalk you?"

"The one and the same, except she's not so young anymore." He clenched his teeth and grunted. "We've got a history. Years ago, in the off-season, I used to go back to Cottage Grove and give lessons to the younger kids. She was one of them. She had a crush on me, but I just saw her as a cute kid. She was funnier than hell, and no matter what life threw at her, she never gave up. Hell, looking back, I wasn't that much older than the kids I was teaching. I think I was around twenty-one years old. It seems like a lifetime ago."

"And…" Bruce sat forward.

"She grew up. Every time I came back from a tournament, I'd tell myself to ignore her and I made sure I was never alone with her."

"Did you go your separate ways?"

"Hell no. She found me wherever I went, even going as far as to make sure the town knew about how much she loved me. I couldn't hurt her. I felt sorry for her. It was just her dad and her. They barely scraped by after her mom ran away. She needed a friend, so I listened to her when she needed to talk. That's all. I didn't mean to encourage her or let her believe that I cared in any other way than as a friend."

Bruce shrugged. "That sounds like you. You're a good friend to others."

"When she turned eighteen, everything changed." He scratched his jaw. "She changed. Suddenly I realized that the little friend that pestered me and kept me in laughs had turned into someone who…she's beautiful, you know."

"How old is she now?"

"Twenty-four, maybe twenty-five." He sighed.

Bruce clicked his tongue. "The age difference isn't such a big obstacle now."

"I shouldn't feel this way about her."

"Why not?" Bruce asked. "You're both adults."

"She might be older, but she's still naive compared to me. I've been on my own my whole life. Even when my parents were alive, they weren't with me. I raised myself, with my manager leading my way." He stared out at the water. "I'm not someone who does the whole dating scene. I can't."

"Why not?"

"I know what she wants. She wants love, marriage, and forever. I don't do any of those. I don't believe in them." He stood up and crossed to the porch railing. "Maybe it's all about the chase. She's the one woman who turned me down, and I hate losing."

Bruce joined him and motioned toward the boat tied up on shore. "Let's go fishing. Maybe once I show you how to hook a fish, you can go back and catch the woman."

Chapter Fifteen

Shauna survived another week of working on the benefit all by herself, and even managed to hide out in the hotel room across the road from the commerce building in her free time. She'd gone out with Kate and Diana, afraid that Diana would somehow find out she was staying in the same hotel she was working at, but neither one of them uttered a single word about what was going on with her family. For all they knew, she was staying at home with her dad and throwing herself into what everyone knew as the Celebrating Cottage Grove event.

The excitement of her secret plan going public on Wednesday helped distract everyone from what was going on in her personal life. For that, she was grateful.

The decision to throw herself into a routine helped take her focus off what was going on with Grayson. She finished her day, went to the hotel, got through the night, and returned to work the next morning. She didn't cry or sleep, and she managed to consume enough food to keep her going. The smile on her face hid the tug of war happening in her heart.

Grayson had left Cottage Grove two weeks ago. The rumors in town swung between Grayson returning to the tennis circuit and him escaping with a woman who'd ended up pregnant from one of his spotlight affairs. Mr. Winston informed her—not that she'd asked—that even the workers at the tennis center were staying silent about their boss's whereabouts.

She opened the front door at the Quayside and stood inside, letting her eyes adjust to the lights. Spotting her friends at the back table, she waved to the host, and then made her way through the room.

John stood up, smiling. "Good. You made it. I was getting ready to call and see if you'd changed your mind."

She walked into his arms. "I told you I would. I just had something I needed to take care of first."

"I'll go get you a drink. Have you eaten?" he asked.

"I'm not hungry. A drink will be fine. Thank you." She sat down.

He left for the bar, and she turned toward Kate. "Is that the new shirt you were talking about?"

"Yep, and it's not the only thing sparkling." Kate held out her hand and waved her fingers. Shauna gasped. A huge solitaire diamond ring glimmered on Kate's slim finger.

"Get out of here!" She grabbed Kate's hand and brought the piece of high-priced jewelry closer. "When did this happen and why didn't you call me?"

"Wednesday, and I tried." Kate stuck her lower lip out. "Your dad said you'd moved out. Where have you been, Shauna?"

Diana leaned forward. "We spent all day calling your cell phone, but it goes to voice mail."

"Diana saw your car at the hotel earlier too." Kate frowned. "You're not having an affair with some married man, are you? Why aren't you at home?"

John slid into his chair, and picked up the last of the conversation. "That's a question that I think we'd all like to have answered. Your friends called me today, thinking I'd know where you were. I know I've been busy the last couple of weeks, but we have talked and you haven't mentioned anything was wrong. I grew concerned when I couldn't get ahold of you last night, and I stopped by your dad's garage this morning. He wouldn't tell me anything, except I'd have to ask you."

"You shouldn't have done that," she whispered, fingering the napkin. "I'm fine. It was always my plan to find my own place, once I had time to look around at the real estate market."

"Shauna, you're staying at the hotel, not an apartment." Kate grasped Shauna's hand. "Why?"

"You do know that we're all here to help you...with anything you need." John reached over and clasped her hand. "You didn't even mention you were having problems when I talked to you while I was in Oregon last week."

"I'm sorry." She gazed down at the table.

How did she explain that the precious hold she had on her life had slipped from her grasp? Not willing to allow them to see how much she was hurting, she squared her shoulders and hoped she could tell them without breaking down.

"Apparently, when I was away at college, my mother decided to come back to my father. This is all a surprise to me. I had no idea until the other day. My dad...well, he kept it a secret from me." She shrugged. "He's happy, I guess, so I figured since I'm an adult I'd give them privacy and find my own place sooner than I planned. With all the hours I'm putting in organizing the Celebrating Cottage Grove event, I haven't found time to go house hunting, or even apartment digging. In the meantime, I'm staying at the hotel."

"Oh, Shauna." Kate pulled her into her arms. "You must be in shock."

"The bitch," Diana hissed. "I'm sorry, I know she's your mom but you can't let her hurt you again. She almost destroyed you the last time she left."

John cleared his throat. "Why don't you stay with me? You'll be more comfortable than at the hotel."

"I couldn't." She leaned over and kissed his cheek. "I'll be fine, really."

He frowned. "I insist. I have a spare bedroom and it'll give you time to understand all the changes you're going through. I really like you, Shauna. I don't want to pressure you, but I want to show you how I'm here for you through the good times and bad. As a friend..."

She glanced around her circle of friends. Kate and Diana

nodded, encouraging her to accept his offer. John was someone she could depend on. He was committed to his business, even tempered, and caring. He was nothing like Grayson who let his power control how he acted. No, John was a giver.

She nodded. "Okay, I'll stay in your spare room, but only until I can find somewhere besides a room at the hotel."

"No hurry." He smiled. "Is there anything you need?"

She scrunched her nose. "I'd like to get the rest of my clothes from the house, but—"

"I'll get them for you." John stood up. "I'll also let your dad know you'll be staying with me. He's worried."

She swallowed. "Thank you."

The moment John slipped out of sight, Kate and Diane attacked. Shauna shook her head and held up her hands. She couldn't answer all their questions at once.

"Kate goes first." She leaned forward. "Two questions from each of you. That's all I'm allowing."

"Fine." Kate grabbed her hand. "Does your mom coming back have anything to do with Grayson leaving town?"

"No."

"Does Grayson's absence have anything to do with you?" Kate lowered her voice. "You can't lie to us."

She swallowed. "Yes. It's my fault he left."

"What happened?"

Shauna held up her hand. "You've already asked your two questions. It's Diane's turn."

"What did he do? I know it wasn't your fault. It never is. He's making you feel guilty again, and that makes me want to kick his ass." Diana clutched her fingers and held up a fist.

"If he did anything, it was making the mistake of asking me to sleep with him. Next question…"

"Shut up. You would never turn him down." Diana narrowed her eyes. "Ever."

"Are you asking?" Shauna slumped back in her chair.

"Yes, dammit. I want to know if you slept with him."

"No," Shauna whispered. "I wanted to, but I couldn't."

"Oh." Diana glanced at Kate. "You mean you were unable to… to physically have sex?"

She inflated her cheeks and blew the air out. "No, that's not what I mean. I can't let myself go there. Not with him."

"Did you turn him down to get even?" Kate rubbed her arm.

She shook her head. "No more questions. I want to hear about your engagement. How did Jackson propose?"

The story went on in front of her, but she couldn't follow along. She smiled and nodded in the right places, but her thoughts drifted back to Grayson. Could he believe she'd told him she wouldn't have sex with him to get back at him?

No, he wouldn't think that way. She would never hurt him to pay him back for all the times he'd ignored her. She slipped her hand into her purse, turned on her phone, and texted Grayson's phone.

I need to talk to you.

There. That's all she could do right now. If he wanted to call her back, the ball was in his court. There was nothing more she could do.

Chapter Sixteen

The long, low wolf whistle came from the end of the hall. Shauna lifted her gaze and laughed. It was strange to be going out on a date with the man you were living with.

"You look gorgeous." John kissed her cheek.

The yellow and turquoise sundress was new, along with the wedged sandals. Yesterday, Kate and Diana had brought over a cake and ice cream to John's house. She hadn't even remembered it was her birthday.

She'd lain awake most of the night wondering what her dad was doing and if he was thinking about her. Even when she was away from home, he'd traveled to Cal State to see her on her birthday.

"We better get going if we're going to make the show." John picked up his car keys.

She followed him outside, and slid into the passenger seat. A wet nose nudged her arm, and she grinned, reaching to scratch the shaggy mutt in the backseat.

"You've either got a stowaway in your car, or this dog's got a hot date too," she said.

"Sit down, Blue." John started the engine. "This one needs a little socialization, so I thought we'd take him with us. You don't mind, do you?"

"Not at all." She smiled. "I love animals. Maybe I'll buy a dog once I find somewhere to live. I never had a pet growing up. I like the idea of having someone always excited to see me when I come home from work. Do you think a dog would be okay by himself during the day? Maybe I should get a cat."

John double glanced at her and grinned. "I don't picture you as a cat lady."

"I said one cat, not six." Shauna slapped his arm. "You're right though. I think I'm more of a dog person. I'll have to give the idea of being a pet owner more thought. It's a big commitment."

When they passed the road to Schyler's Tennis Center, she forced herself to keep her eyes on the road. She'd heard Grayson was back, but his whereabouts no longer concerned her. She reached over and slipped her hand into John's.

He squeezed her fingers. "Have you heard what movie they're playing at the park?"

"*Back to the Future.* The first one." She groaned. "I think I've seen it about twelve times over the years."

"That's okay." He leaned over and snuck a quick kiss. "I'm sure we can keep ourselves entertained in other ways."

Warmth filled her, and she relaxed. John had surprised her during the week and had kept his word on not rushing her into a relationship she wasn't emotionally ready for, but she'd found herself wanting to please him. It was nice to come back to his house after working and he listened as she talked about her day.

He hadn't pushed her to go further than a few kisses. She let him think the reason for her hesitation was because of her mom being back in town. To explain about Grayson and her own feelings was something she wasn't ready to deal with yet.

Once in town, they found a parking spot a block from the main street and walked toward the park. Shauna took Blue's leash from John and slipped her hand into his. The late summer breeze blew her hair off her neck, and she slowed her pace. A crowd had already gathered on the grass, and she waved to several people she recognized.

The Ladies of the Library Association played movies at the park on Saturday nights all throughout the summer for the community. The tradition had started when Shauna had gone away to school. The excitement of the crowd rejuvenated Blue, and he tugged at the leash. She tugged on John's hand to keep up with her as she let Blue have the lead.

The happy spirit flowing in the park was exactly what she wanted for the Celebrating Cottage Grove event. A positive direction on bringing a community together was the main priority. Together, they could accomplish the goal of reviving the town.

Cottage Grove was a small town where people lived their whole lives, and today the multigenerational families were still going strong. Grandparents sat with grandchildren. Parents visited with other adults, and groups of children ran amok.

Blue stuck his black nose up in the air and barked. Shauna stopped and kneeled down. She'd watched John numerous times reward one of the dogs when they'd given a warning bark.

"Good boy." She stood back up. "What kind of dog is Blue?"

"He's part Border Collie. The rest we'll probably never know." John shifted the blanket he carried and pointed. "Let's go sit over there."

Underneath an oak tree, they sat on the quilt and settled Blue in between them. The sun hovered on the horizon. Across the open area stood a large homemade screen made up of several white bed sheets. Shauna waved to Ella who was standing by the picnic table where Mayor Carson was selling bags of popcorn for fifty cents.

"There's Kate and Jackson." John whistled to grab their attention, and then motioned them over.

Shauna smiled and patted the blanket beside her as they approached. "There's room for more. Sit with us."

"Thanks." Kate lowered herself to the ground and squeezed Shauna's hand before whispering, "How are you?"

"Fine." She brushed off the question and turned to Jackson. "Hey, stranger."

Jackson, all five foot eleven inches of him, leaned over Kate and hugged Shauna. "It's good to see you back in town. Sorry I didn't get a chance to talk to you at mom and dad's party a few weeks back. Kate's been after me to join you girls for a night out, but duty calls."

"How do you like working for your dad?" Shauna asked.

Jackson's family owned Trident Oil Company. He'd grown up in Cottage Grove and everyone in town had always known he would assume his dad's role and someday take over the business.

Jackson winked. "About as much as I liked following the rules he laid out when I was a teenager. I keep trying to convince him it's time to retire, but dad's going to dictate what I do his whole life."

Shauna laughed. "I take it you two still butt heads and love every minute of it?"

"Yeah." He grinned. "Now that my brother Stewart is married, at least dad's eased off on me and placing his attention on Stewart and Jill. They just announced they're going to have a baby."

"Wow, congratulations, Uncle Jackson." Shauna grinned.

"Hey, do you two want to go load up on snacks before the movie starts?" Kate scooted closer to Shauna. "I've got the munchies."

"Popcorn and candy bars coming up." John pushed himself to his feet. "Diet drinks for you girls?"

"Oh, you did not just insinuate that we *need* diet drinks." Kate glared.

"Uh…" John glanced to Jackson, who shrugged and backed up, shaking his head. "No, of course not."

Kate elbowed Shauna and they both laughed. The men made a hasty exit. Shauna petted Blue, who tried to follow John.

"You're terrible." Shauna snorted. "Watch him bring us back extra popcorn and pop to make up for that comment."

Kate turned her head, and leaned closer. "Never mind about that. I needed to get them away so I could tell you that Grayson's here."

She nodded. "I know. I heard he'd come back."

"No. I mean he's here at the park," Kate said.

It took Shauna a moment to let the new information soak in. When it did, she forced herself to shrug. "I don't care."

Kate squinted and studied her. "Hm."

"What?"

"I guess I never thought I'd see the day that you got over Grayson Schyler. It's a little hard to believe."

She gazed over at John, walking back toward them. "I'm with John now. He makes me happy."

"I'm glad." Kate scooted over and helped the men pass out the treats. "This better be diet pop, John."

He paused. "It is, but Jackson was the one who ordered the drinks. I'm innocent."

"Smart man. You learn fast." Kate laughed.

"What? You're not mad at Jackson?" John huffed. "Women."

They soon grew quiet and the projector lit up the screen. Shauna snuggled beside John and leaned back against him. The movie distracted the others and with the cover of darkness, she squeezed her eyes shut for a moment. What was Grayson doing here? Had he brought one of his women? Not that it mattered. She had John now.

Before she knew it, intermission came, and Blue stood beside her, wiggling his rear end. She scratched Blue's neck. "Do you need to go for a walk?"

"I'll take him." John shifted to rise, but she patted his leg.

"I'll do it. My foot's asleep, and my butt's numb from sitting on the ground." She stood up, shook her leg, and then limped away until the feeling came back to her foot.

Not wanting Blue to do his job where everyone walked, she hurried to the other end of the park where she knew there were supplied sacks for dog pickups. She continued walking, letting out the retractable leash and giving Blue enough distance to run ahead. When she thought she'd walked a good distance away from the crowd, she moved over to a statue and leaned against it.

Without the benefit of lights in the area, she didn't let Blue go too far away. It was hard enough to see in the dark, she didn't want to lose him if he slipped out of his collar. Alone, she stuck out her lower lip and blew the hair out of her eyes. She was tired of the direction her life was taking her.

She wanted to talk to her dad, but had no desire to deal with the reasons why her mom had decided to reappear in her life. Even at work, she stayed alert in case Grayson showed up, and then beat herself up for doing so. At least throwing herself into organizing the event helped her stay sane.

"Hey, Blue." She patted her leg, and smiled as Blue came running to her. "You're such a good boy. I might just have to steal you away from John. We could hit the road and escape all this nonsense, huh? I'd even let you stick your head out the window. We could listen to loud music, eat junk food, and find us some swanky resort to stay in."

Blue barked.

"What male could turn down an offer like that?" A familiar husky voice spoke behind her.

She stiffened. Every nerve in her body sizzled, and the air in her lungs swelled.

Grayson stepped in front of her. "Hello, Shauna."

Chapter Seventeen

In the two weeks of Grayson's absence, he'd somehow become even sexier. His hair lay mussed, falling down on his forehead. The lines on his forehead were more prominent, and to make it worse, he stood in front of her with his hands deep in the front pockets of his jeans, unthreatening and approachable.

"I need to get back. The movie has probably started." She tugged on Blue's leash, but Grayson leaned down and swept up the pooch.

"You've seen the movie before." He stroked the dog's back, while seeming to gauge her reaction.

"That's not the point. I came with John." She pursed her lips.

She couldn't yank the dog out of his arms. She wasn't heartless. Not stomping away had everything to do with Blue's position, not because Grayson had sought her out.

"I went on vacation." Grayson stepped closer.

Shauna moved backward, bumped into the statue, and groaned. Rubbing the back of her head, she glared when Grayson chuckled.

"Are you sinking to a new low? You not only want to hurt my feelings, but like a little physical pain on me too?"

He shook his head before motioning with his chin for her to look up. She leaned back and tilted her head, and instant recognition came with the dawning realization there was no running away from Grayson Schyler. But it didn't take a ten-foot gold statue of him to knock sense into her brain.

"You're such an ass." She crossed her arms.

"Yeah." He lifted his shoulder and grinned. "Let's go back to my place."

She couldn't keep going on this way, hot one minute, cold the next, and yet Grayson dangled her out of reach while plucking her heartstrings when the mood hit him. She'd had enough. Not willing to let him have control over her, she gently scooped Blue out of his arms and faced Grayson head on.

"I know this is hard to believe, but I've changed. I'm not hanging around Cottage Grove hoping for a little attention. I'm not naïve enough to believe for one minute you feel anything for me, except pity." Her laugh came out harsh and pained even to her own ears. "I'm not a form of entertainment for you when you become bored with your private horde of women. So, if you'll excuse me, I have a man waiting for his dog and his girlfriend and for my answer on whether I'm ready to take our relationship further."

She took two steps, turned back around, and pointed to the doggy bag station behind him. "Oh, by the way, I think Blue left you a gift at the base of your golden statue. You might want to pick that up."

She whirled around. Each step away from Grayson gave her more confidence. She held her head high and marched straight back toward the others, not stopping until she'd reached John. He scrambled to his feet and clutched her arms.

"What happened? Are you okay?"

She smiled. "I'm perfect. Let's go home."

It only took two seconds for him to read the need in her eyes, and he wrapped his arm around her waist and started walking.

"Hey!" Kate raised her head off Jackson's lap. "Where are you going now?"

"Home." She grinned. "I'm tired of my stagnant life, and I'm going to change directions. I'll call you tomorrow."

In less time than she imagined, John pulled up in front of the one-story ranch house and ushered her inside. She stood in the middle of the living room, waiting for him to come back after he secured Blue in the outdoor kennel. For a split second, she debated whether to slip out the front door, hop in her car, and drive away.

A door shut in the rear of the house, and before she could talk herself into following her instincts, John entered the room. She rubbed her arms, warming herself up. Usually summer nights in the low coastal mountains were rather muggy, but she couldn't shake the chill.

"Did Blue protest having to go back in with the other dogs?" she asked.

"No. He was worn out." He embraced her. "You've made me a happy man, deciding to come back here early. I hope I'm not misreading what you want to happen between us."

"I really like you, John." She slipped her arms over his shoulders and gazed into his eyes. "I've been unfair, and you've been more patient than I expected."

"You're worth it."

She opened, and then closed her mouth. Was she? She'd failed her dad, her mother, and she couldn't even satisfy Grayson to save her life.

"Did I say something wrong?" he asked.

Shauna sucked in a breath. "No."

She'd gone over the reasons why getting involved with John was a good thing. Yet she couldn't stop thinking about Grayson and apparently it would take drastic measures to make her forget how Grayson made her feel when he touched her.

She leaned in and kissed John. On the mouth. Slow, and lingering.

The warm pressure of his lips promised her a night to remember. In the war of emotions going on inside her soul, doing what was right, what felt good, what she needed, was winning.

She pressed her breasts against his chest. She enjoyed the way his body comforted her, and in startling surprise, the way he reacted helped her feel complete, real, desired.

He broke the kiss, and rested his chin on the top of her head, holding her to his chest. His heart raced against her cheek, and she closed her eyes. John brought out the good things in her, and she wanted to please him.

She rubbed his back, gaining confidence, exploring, until her hands rested on the top of his jeans, pulling him closer. He groaned, lifting her face and heating things up. His tongue brushed the inside of her lip and she jerked back with the speed of an activated mousetrap. Frozen in place, she dared not breathe, or he'd pounce.

Seconds ticked by without either of them moving.

"Aw, Shauna." He reached for her, but she moved back, her hand automatically going to her throat.

"I–I'm sorry." She swallowed past the horror of what she'd done.

He sighed and shook his head sadly. "Don't be. I knew my feelings for you exceeded how you felt about me. I told myself to wait, to let you learn that we could be good together, but it's not true, is it? There'll never be an us."

She blinked to clear her vision, and was surprised at how the tears wouldn't stop. "I wanted it to be different. I tried. I really did, but…"

He ran his hand through his hair. "But you love Grayson."

She dropped her gaze to the carpet and nodded.

"He doesn't deserve you."

"I know."

"I care about you. I only want what is best."

"I know."

"What happens if he never wises up and realizes how much you love him?"

She lifted her chin. "I don't know."

John hesitated, and then cleared his throat. "Will you be all right?"

"Eventually." She attempted to smile, and failed.

"Okay." He motioned toward the hallway. "I'll leave you alone. If you need me, you know where I'll be."

She watched him walk away, her heart sinking to the pit of her stomach. "John?"

He stopped and turned. "Yeah?"

"Thank you."

He smiled tenderly, nodded his acceptance, and walked out of sight.

Chapter Eighteen

Ella hustled into the office, closed the door, and planted herself in front of the exit. "Shauna, we'll need the press kits from everybody in two weeks."

Shauna frowned. "Okay."

Her secretary's flushed face and rapid breathing had nothing to do with the message. Shauna had already emailed the updated notices to Grayson, and he'd replied that he'd pass the message on.

"What's with you? Did Herbert Kendall come in again?" Shauna shut off her computer.

"No," Ella said. "I haven't seen him all week."

Herbert's habitual complaining about the city often flustered the even-tempered woman, until Shauna intervened on Ella's behalf, promising to talk to the city council on his behalf. She removed her purse out of the bottom drawer of her desk, and then stepped around, ready to follow Ella out of the office.

"You can't leave." Ella widened her stance.

"Why not?"

"They're spraying for bugs." Ella crossed her arms.

"At six o'clock? I don't think so." Shauna shook her head and made to walk around Ella, but Ella grabbed her arms.

"Tell me what size advertisement you want in next week's paper." Ella's brows rose. "Do we want to go with color or black and white?"

"Enough, Ella." Shauna laughed and moved the stubborn woman aside. "I don't know what's going on with you, but I have somewhere I need to go. It's already an hour past closing time. We've gone over everything we need to today, but I promise if you're that confused we can go over it all again on Monday."

"Fine." Ella blew out her breath. "Just don't fire me."

"I think you need to go home, relax, and maybe go out for a few drinks. You seem stressed, and you know I'd never get rid of you." Shauna smiled. "You work too hard and keep me focused. I'd be lost without you."

With that said, she opened the door, turned left, and proceeded to the back of the building. Determined to make things right with her dad, she headed toward the street where she'd parked her car.

If she were lucky, her dad would still be in the garage working and she'd be able to have the conversation she should've had with him a long time ago. She'd been ignoring the fact her mom was back for the indefinite future and if she got this over with, she'd sleep better at night.

Her mom could go to hell for all she cared, but her dad had always been there for her. He'd scrimped for years to put her through college, even letting her live on campus when she knew he'd have to work longer hours to foot the bill. When her teen years became unbearable, no one was better at holding her while she cried and teaching her to stand up for herself.

He'd never left her and for that reason alone, she'd figure out how to make their father-daughter relationship work.

She rounded the corner and came to a complete stop. Every thought erased from her mind at the sight of Grayson leaning against her car. The hair stood up on her nape, and despite how much she tried to ignore the happiness bubbling inside of her, she couldn't control the way her stomach flip-flopped.

"What do you want?"

"You."

She walked around the front of the car, keeping space between Grayson and herself. "I get it, Grayson. You want to make my life miserable the way I did to you. Fine. Whatever. Let me repay you back. I will not now, or ever, sleep with you. Now you can go on with your life and forget all about me, because that's what I did.

You're not even a bleep on my radar. See how good it works."

He moved over and held her door shut, not letting her climb in and drive away. "What's wrong?"

"Nothing."

"Bullshit." He lowered his voice. "I can see it in your eyes."

She blinked. "It doesn't matter."

"Whatever you think about me, I do care about you." He stroked her arm. "Maybe too much, and that's the problem."

"Grayson…" She sighed, her determination not to fall for his pretty words fading with each second. "I need to go do something. My problems have nothing to do with you. You're just the unlucky person who stepped into my path today."

"Talk to me." He lifted her chin. "You used to trust me with what was going on in your life. I'd like to help."

"So you say, but where were you when I needed you a few weeks ago? You talk big, but so far I haven't seen that part of you who used to be friends with me. You're hard and cold. I don't even know you anymore." She sniffed. Dammit, she was not going to cry.

"When did you come to me?"

"The night I went to your house and made an absolute fool out of myself. Later, I'd gone back to talk to you, to take you up on your offer, and you were gone. Now it's too late. Everything has changed."

"No, it hasn't. I've been an ass, but I want to make it up to you." He framed his hands around her face. "Go do what you have to do, and then I'll come over to your house and we can talk. Just talk."

She shook her head. "I'm not staying with my dad anymore."

"Okay." He frowned. "Come to my house. Please."

She hesitated. Was she asking for disappointment again? When would she ever say enough is enough?

"Miss Marino!" Mrs. Bakkersten shuffled across the street and approached them, out of breath. "I'm so glad I found you, dear. Your dad's been trying to get a hold of you."

She reached out toward Grayson. "What's wrong?"

"He's been trying to call you for the last hour." Mrs. Bakkersten tsked and shook her head. "He asked me to find you, and since everyone knows you're living back at the hotel after your breakup with John, that was the first place I looked. I'm lucky to find you here."

Grayson pulled her tight against his side. "Wait, you broke up with John?"

"Never mind that…" She pressed her fingers into her temple. "Did something happen? Is my dad hurt?"

Visions of a lift malfunctioning and her dad pinned under a vehicle stole her breath.

Mrs. Bakkersten grabbed Shauna's hand. "No, dear, but he said it was very important. He wants you to call his cell phone."

She blew her breath out. *He's not hurt. He's okay.*

"Thank you." Shauna leaned against Grayson's side, letting him hold her against him.

"You're welcome." Mrs. Bakkersten glanced back and forth between Grayson and Shauna. "I expect better out of you this time, Mr. Schyler. Don't you go breaking this young thing's heart, or sleeping with all those other women you enjoy parading around everywhere. Shauna has always loved you, and doesn't deserve the way you treat her."

Grayson grinned and nodded. "Yes, ma'am. I'll be careful."

The older woman drilled him with one last condescending look and then harrumphed, pivoting on her two-inch heels and marching back across the street. Shauna shook her head.

"You've got some supporters in town." Grayson chuckled.

Aware of how she was pressing her body against him, she stepped back and dug her phone out of her purse. She could've sworn she'd turned the phone on this morning, but the display wouldn't light up. *Dammit.*

"Here. You can use mine." Grayson held out his phone.

"Thanks." She punched in the number and paced, while she waited for her dad to pick up.

"Hey, dad. It's me."

"Buddy, you need to come over right away. This has gone on long enough," Tony said.

Her back stiffened. Not one who particularly enjoyed having someone order her around, she hesitated before telling him she was on her way over now.

"Your mom's packing." He cursed under his breath. "She says she doesn't want to come between us anymore, and is leaving."

"Dad...this doesn't involve me." She clamped her lips together briefly. "If she wants to leave, let her go. Besides, she's left before and we were fine without her."

The conversation died. Shauna waited, surprised to find her hands shaking. There were too many things going on in her life to worry about the feelings of a woman who'd given her own child no thought when she'd hightailed it out of town.

"Shauna." Tony cleared his throat. "Do it for me. Come talk to your mother."

"She's not what I would call a mother, dad," she said.

"I know you believe that but you don't know...just come over, please. I love her." Tony hung up.

Shauna pulled the phone away from her ear, stared at it in shock, and then cocked her arm back to throw it when Grayson grabbed her hand, rescuing his phone. She glared at him.

"I would've bought you a new one." She jerked her arm.

"That's not the point." He slid the phone in his back pocket.

"It never is with you." She stomped away.

She wanted to hit something, or smash a window. Anger rolled up her back and she flung her arms out to the sides. "What is with people? They think they can manipulate and threaten whenever they want, and if it gets too tough...bam! They're gone, leaving their shit behind and not giving another thought to anyone else."

"I don't—"

"It's sickening! I wish she'd leave. I don't want her here. Everything was fine before she came back. Dad was happy. I was happy. We don't need her." She swung her foot out and kicked the hubcap on her car. Pain radiated up her toes to her ankle. "Dammit!"

She limped to the driver's side door, flung it open, and threw in her purse. All the stress, confusion, and heartache she'd suffered through coiled into an angry ball in the pit of her stomach, and she rounded on Grayson.

"You're no better than my mother." She poked him in the chest, backing him toward the middle of the street. "You dangled me like...like one of your airheaded blonds who kiss your ass and don't care that in the morning you'll be gone. Well, guess what? I take back every second I wasted hoping and praying that you'd wake up and see how much I lo—"

He moved forward, making her retreat, walking with that lazy long stride that had the ability to hypnotize her. His gaze was so intent, her breasts hardened and she forgot why she was wasting her time arguing. His hair lay over his forehead in a sexy I-don't-give-a-damn way that tempted her to reach up and sweep it back. But she didn't. She couldn't get that close. Not the way her body sang when he was near.

The back of her thighs hit against the car, her breath barely coming through the constant throb of her body. "What are you doing?"

"I'm going to take what's mine." He lowered his head, hovering inches from her mouth. "I don't care if I get it here, in the middle of Main Street, or if you come over to my house and let me have you there. But I'll be damned if we're gonna pussy foot around this subject any longer."

"But..."

He shook his head. "I'm done fighting, Shauna. I want you. You hear me? I want you as much as you want me. For as long as you want me."

Oh my God. She forgot to breathe. She'd waited forever to hear him admit his feelings toward her, to confess it wasn't her imagination dreaming up a future with him. Everyone thought her crush was one sided, but she knew better. She sucked in air, filling her lungs.

Then the magnitude of her dad's phone call hit her. She stumbled backward.

"My mom…" She pressed her fingers against her forehead. "My mom's back, Grayson. Why did she come back?"

"Aw, sweetheart." He gathered her in his arms.

His body was warm, and she leaned forward. Her body strained against her clothing while her head warned her that they were out in plain view of anyone who was downtown.

"You're not alone. I'm here. You have friends." He stroked the hair back from her face. "I'll help you."

"How do I know you're telling me the truth?" She gazed up into his eyes. "I don't want to turn back into the person I was, Grayson. I don't want to hurt inside anymore."

"There was never anything wrong with you before." He kissed her forehead. "I understood you."

"But you're so angry."

"You painted my name all over town." He grinned. "I get angry. It's what we do."

She laughed softly. "We're screw-ups."

"Yep." He expelled his breath in a whoosh. "Let's start over. Come to my house."

She nodded. "I'll come over."

"No pressure. I'm not a jerk. I had no idea what else you were going through. Sweetheart, you have a lot going on. I'm sorry. If I'd have known, I wouldn't have left town." He studied her.

She gazed up at him. "We can talk."

"Promise?"

"Y-yes." She rolled her eyes. "After I go talk to my dad."

He lifted his hand and traced a finger over her bottom lip. "Hurry."

She sighed, and gave him a half smile. *I will.*

Chapter Nineteen

Shauna scrambled out of her car and hurried up the walkway to her dad's house, her heels clicking rapidly on the concrete. The house looked the same as it had the day she'd left. The lawn still needed mowing, and dad's overalls still hung at the end of the porch in their usual place.

As she negotiated the steps and crossed to the front door, she paused, steeling herself for what was to come. She planned to support her dad the same way she's always backed him.

She knocked, and let herself in. "Dad?"

Tony stood up from the couch. His thinning hair stood out from his head and there were grease marks smeared across his wrinkled forehead, showing her how many times he'd ran his hand through his hair. A sign that his frustration level was about to explode.

She walked into his arms and let him hold her tight. His chest trembled and he squeezed her tighter. She swallowed the growing lump in her throat.

"I missed you, buddy." He stepped back, planted his hands on her shoulders, and sniffed. "I'm so glad you're here. You belong here. This is your home."

She smiled sadly. "It's okay. I'm doing fine on my own. You made sure I was capable of standing on my own two feet."

He sighed and reached into his front shirt pocket before dropping his empty hand. A former smoker, he still reached for the cigarette pack he expected to be there when times were rough.

"What's going on, dad?"

"She's leaving me again," he said.

"Did you really expect her to stay? She's good at walking away and not looking back." She crossed her arms and softened her voice. "I hate that she's hurting you."

"Don't say that." Tony frowned. "I didn't raise you to talk bad about your mother, and I won't put up with it now, in my own home."

She clamped her lips shut. Her continual hatred for her mother had remained a sore spot between them for years, and one she tried hard not to verbalize aloud when her dad was near. "Anything you need, I'll help. If you want me to move back, I will. I'll even cook your dinners and spend time assisting you in the garage, if you want to start going out and having a good time. You work too hard…"

"All I want you to do is talk with her." Tony seemed to gain confidence once he'd spoken the words. "She's leaving because she knows I'm upset and worried about you."

Shauna snorted and turned around. She walked over to the mantle and straightened the picture Mr. Gunderson, the school photographer, had snapped of her in seventh grade during the father and daughter dance. *Oh dad, how could you still love her?*

"I've never stopped wanting her to come home. Even when she was gone and I thought I'd never see her again, I never stopped hoping and praying." Tony cleared his throat. "I thought I would die without her, but I didn't. Because of you. I can't explain how much having her back here with me makes me feel alive—"

Shauna glanced over her shoulder. "She didn't love you enough. Real love doesn't work that way."

Tony hung his head and whispered, "Real love is different for everyone, Shauna."

At that moment, she'd do anything to see her strong, stubborn father stand up proudly and order her to go to her room. It broke her heart to see him weakened by a woman who never gave a damn how she hurt others.

"Fine." Shauna stepped in front of her dad and rubbed his arms. "I'll talk to her."

He mouthed the words thank you.

"I love you, dad."

"I love you, too." He kissed her forehead. "She's up in our bedroom."

She noticed it wasn't *his* bedroom anymore. When had it changed? When had life become so complicated? When would they ever heal from the pain Belinda brought them?

The kind of love her dad talked about was something she never wanted to experience. It hadn't taken her long after her mom left to know that when she found someone to love, it would be the forever kind. The kind of love that never wavers and no matter what, you never give up.

No one, not even Kate and Diana, knew the reasons she'd never given up on loving Grayson. They would never understand that if she threw it all away, she'd be no better than her mom. She wasn't stupid. At one time, her love had been forced and a figment of her imagination, but the night she'd taken matters into her own hands and thrown her naked self at him, she'd known that her crush had turned into something more. She'd seen the need in Grayson's eyes, and his denial couldn't beat that.

If someone asked her to explain how that happens, she'd have no words. They'd shared a look. She and Grayson had seen the truth. They'd connected on a level deeper than she'd seen two people achieve. And tonight, Grayson had proven that she wasn't crazy. He felt it too.

She knocked on the bedroom door, and walked in without waiting for an answer. Belinda sat on the edge of the bed, a ball of toilet paper wadded up in her hand. She dabbed her eyes, and stood up. Shauna closed the door, glancing away from her mother.

"Shauna?"

She nodded. "I've come to tell you that I'm okay with you staying at the house. I've got my own place, or I will soon."

"This is your home. Your dad wants you here." Belinda stood up. "I want you here."

Shauna schooled her reaction. "Dad and I are fine. That's something that'll never change no matter where I am."

"I know, but I want…" She approached Shauna. "I want to get to know you."

Shauna stood up straighter. She stood a few inches taller than her mom, and she wondered when that'd happened. Last time she'd seen her, she was still young enough to crawl onto her lap and enjoy her mother's comfort.

"Gosh, I'm swamped at work with the fundraiser in two weeks, and I have to find time to interview a realtor to work with. Not to mention I have an active social life." She shrugged. "Now's not a great time to start something new."

"Shauna. Please." Belinda reached out, surprising Shauna with the firm grip on her arm. "There are things I'd like to explain. I know you're mad. You have every reason to hate me, but I need to do this for myself."

Shauna shook her head in disbelief. "It's always about you, isn't it? You want to give me an excuse for why you stopped loving me, so you can go on lying to my dad and eventually kill him?"

"No," Belinda said. "I don't want to hurt you or him. There are reasons why I left and stayed away."

"You know what?" She blew her breath out and smiled. "It doesn't matter. It seems you're back. That's great. Dad's accepted you. Even better. You want to prove you don't want to hurt him? Then stay here and make him happy. Leaving him is only going to hurt him more."

Belinda nodded. "I'll stay."

"Great." She turned and walked through the door.

"Shauna."

She stopped, but refused to turn around.

"I'd like to talk to you…someday soon."

Shauna glanced over her shoulder. "I guess I'm more like you than I realized. It doesn't hurt me to walk away from you."

On the way out of the house, she kissed her dad and told him she loved him. He never stopped her from leaving, and she never looked back. She had someone waiting for her, and she would not disappoint him. That was what real love was all about.

Chapter Twenty

The cooler air outside Grayson's home, underneath the canopy of trees, kissed her overheated skin. Her steps faltered. Grayson was leaning against the doorframe, the same intense expression written on his face that he'd had earlier.

Except, he'd removed his shirt and shoes, and the sight of him barefooted, wearing only his shorts, had her imagining what it would be like to finally see his hard body naked, with nothing between them. She slowed down, suddenly nervous. He was a lot of man to take in all at once, especially when he focused all his attention on her.

A small grin curled the sides of his mouth and she moved forward. She needed him. Now. So she could validate her feelings. So she could move on. So she could tell him how much she loved him.

"Are you okay, Shauna?"

His voice, soft yet gravelly, rode over her, caressing her skin. The nerves in her stomach flittered, sending shivers throughout her body. Not once had she strayed from her feelings when it came to him. Oh, she'd tried everything she could think of to stop loving him. There were a handful of boyfriends in college and lately, John, but deep down she'd used each one of them to try to forget about Grayson. It never worked. Grayson was the one she wanted.

"I'm wonderful." She didn't stop until she was in front of him, and then she wrapped her arms around his neck and kissed him for all it was worth.

When she thought she'd pass out from lack of oxygen, she kissed her way down to the hollow of his throat. The heat of his skin, mixed with the slight taste of salt, warmed her insides and she pressed against him.

Her tongue darted out and stroked his collarbone. Grayson groaned and swept her up in his arms. She continued exploring his body as he carried her up the stairs and laid her on the bed.

He hovered over her, staring down at her. She stretched, reaching for him.

"You know what you're doing." A slow smile came to his lips.

"Mmhm." She nodded. She knew they were different people. He was famous and rich. She was a determined small town girl. But their wants were the same. They both needed each other.

The chemistry between them exploded whenever they were around each other. If she was going to break through the hard shell he kept his heart in, she'd have to prove to him, tonight, that she was worth loving.

Her legs loosened, and she arched. Every cell in her body pleaded for more. She wanted to touch every part of his body. She knew when they did come together, they'd fit perfectly. He was her missing part. They belonged together.

She slipped her finger between his hard stomach and the waistband of his shorts, and slowly dragged them down. His breath grew ragged, and she looked into his eyes as her fingers wrapped around his hardness. Surprised when he grew even larger in her hand, she arched her pelvis up, wanting him inside her.

The way his arms quivered to hold himself off her and keep himself in check had her smiling. She pressed her hand against his chest, his heart beating wildly in her palm, and she smiled. She was right. No words were necessary.

"Roll over," she whispered.

He took her with him, until he was flat on his back with her straddling his thighs. A thrum of excitement at the new position encouraged her to go on. She crossed her arms, grabbed the hem of her blouse, and removed it over her head. She tossed her hair behind her back, wiggling her skirt bunched around her waist. The thong she wore left every inch of her bare to feel the heat coming off him.

"Jesus…" Grayson ran his hands up her flat stomach and cupped her breasts. "You're beautiful."

With him, she wasn't an innocent. She'd made love to him in her imagination many times, and knew how the night would end. Yet, really being here, being with him, was different than she'd ever dreamed. The heady sense of control and the powerful way her body responded was something new. Her hips instinctively shifted, seeking him. The pressure built within her body, urging her on.

"I want you inside of me." She rubbed against him, enjoying the way he teased her body into accepting him.

"Let me enjoy you." He rolled her nipples between his thumb and finger. "You're shaking."

"I need you." She arched back, trembling. "All of you."

He settled her on top of his hardness. She moaned. The heat coming off him singed her skin and pleasure shot through her.

"Grayson…" She panted. "Please."

"God, I like when you beg." His gaze darkened.

He slipped one hand down between them, and in a move that left her gasping for breath, swept the thin slip of material to the side and positioned the head of his erection into her moistness. She held herself still, wanting, needing, but hesitant to plunge herself onto him. He moaned and gripped her hips with his experienced hands, thrusting off the bed and filling her completely. She gasped and froze.

Grayson's gaze lifted to her face and darkened. "Dammit, Shauna."

She might not have expected the way her body reacted to all the new feelings, but she'd presumed he knew that she'd waited for her first time to be with him. His hardness pulsed inside of her, and she swallowed. Her body tightened around him, and the sharp intrusion gave way to a pleasant fullness. New sensations she had no control over sparked to life. She moved atop him, hesitantly at first, pleased when Grayson clenched his teeth together and sucked in his breath.

Growing more daring, she lifted and moved back and forth, up and down on him. Grayson's eyes closed and his jaw quivered. She sprawled her fingers on his chest, leveraging herself. Her body vibrated with growing excitement.

Grayson opened his eyes, now sleepy with passion. He ran a single finger between her cleavage and flicked open the front clasp on her bra. Her breasts spilled out, leaving them exposed to his eyes, to his hands, and she moaned as he cupped, molded, and caressed.

"Oh God." She bit down on her lower lip and sped up her movements, straining for what she knew would be the biggest gift of all, but was dangling right out of her reach.

He leaned forward, propping himself on his elbows, and took one of her nipples in his mouth. Waves of intense need pounded inside of her with each stroke of his tongue, each gentle suck of his lips. The spasms drew a long cry of pleasure from her lips, as the zenith exploded from deep inside her core and left her completely limp.

Grayson rolled her back over, until he was above her, planted deep in her body. He closed his eyes and plunged inside of her with a groan of completion, holding himself still as tremors racked his body.

What seemed like hours, but what were really mere seconds later, they both gazed at each other as the magnitude of what had just happened struck them both. She lifted her arms, but he pulled out of her and moved off the bed, keeping his back to her.

"Grayson?" She sat up.

He scooped his shorts off the floor and slipped them on. "Don't."

The ice coming off that one word froze her to the bed. She recoiled from his anger, and watched him walk away. Everything she'd ignored in her life came crashing down on her and she curled on the bed, wrapping her arms around her knees. She stared, dried eyed, at the white wall. He should've known she could never give herself to anyone but him.

Chapter Twenty-One

Shauna was sleeping when Grayson came back inside a couple hours later. Her lashes lay still on her cheeks. The act of having sex came back with crystal clarity and wounded him. He couldn't blame her. This time, he'd asked her to come to the house with one thing on his mind.

The truth was, he'd known he should walk away—for her sake. But he'd wanted her too much. He was a selfish bastard.

In the dim light coming through the window from the floodlight over the garage, he could see what he'd done. He'd taken her generosity, her idea of love, her goodness, and used her in a way he did every other woman in his life.

She had no indication that what he'd planned had no weight on their relationship. He was Grayson Schyler, playboy and sworn bachelor. Love, even a long-term relationship, was out of the question.

Who am I fooling?

Tonight was more than a mutual satisfaction between the sheets. Somewhere behind the primal, physical need to have Shauna, he'd recognized hope within himself. A desire to feel complete and understood by the one person he wanted more than anything. A dream he thought he'd buried a long time ago. His wish was there, waiting, right below the surface, wanting to come true.

He sank down beside her on the mattress, not touching her warm, willing body. He might never experience what he had with her again, but he was too selfish to walk away. He'd only lie beside her for a couple minutes, and then he'd leave.

Sometime later, he opened his eyes, surprised to have drifted off into sleep. For a moment, he had to remember where he was at and what had happened. He stroked the arm thrown over his stomach, and relaxed. He was home, and Shauna was with him. Then the reality of what had happened came back. He'd taken her virginity.

He scooted out from under her, hoping to have a few moments to wake up and think. He had to practice what he would say to her.

"Gray...?" She brought her hands up to her face and rubbed her eyes, smiling at finding him beside the bed. "Come back to bed."

"You fooled me."

She flinched and sat up. Grayson stood, fully dressed, and glared.

"What are you talking about?" She scooted toward the edge of the bed and stood. His gaze heated as he took in all her bare skin before marching over to the dresser, removing a T-shirt, and tossing it to her.

"Get dressed, and then come down to the kitchen. We need to talk."

"What's going on?" She slipped the shirt over her head, letting the material fall to the top of her thighs. "Are you angry at me?"

He ignored her questions. His head pounded, and he had to put a distance between them. He couldn't do that while she was standing in his bedroom.

He stepped backward, putting space between them. "I'm going downstairs. Come down when you're ready."

"Is this some kind of test? Did I fail?" She hugged her middle, shivering.

"No. It wasn't a...test." He gritted his teeth, and walked out of the room.

Five minutes later, she showed up downstairs. He handed her a cup of coffee, and motioned for her to sit across from him at the table.

She sat. "You're scaring me."

"Good." He returned to his place, and leaned his elbows against the table. "Shauna…"

He watched her, knowing he was going to break her heart. She placed her hands between her legs and waited.

He lifted his head, miserable. There were many things he regretted in his life, but hurting Shauna topped the charts. She had no idea how much it pained him to constantly cause her more disappointment.

"Oh God." She covered her mouth and shook her head. "You're going to walk away from me."

"I'm sorry." He reached across the table for her hand and waited until she placed her fingers into his palm. "I had no idea you'd never slept with anyone before."

She frowned. "How could you not? It's always been you who I've wanted. Always."

He physically flinched. "I don't deserve you. You're looking for a man who will come home every evening and hold you in bed until you both fall asleep. I'm…the exact opposite. I don't want to answer to anyone or be responsible for your happiness. I can't. I won't."

"What are you saying?" She rubbed her lips together. "Are you denying what we have together? Is it because of my past?"

"No. Hell no." He let go of her and leaned back. "Even back then, I admired your tenacity. Then all of a sudden, you grew up and I reacted. You drove me crazy with wanting you, but I knew there could be nothing between us. My world involved traveling and the tournaments. The media would've crushed you and even though I was attracted to you, I pushed you away the only way I knew how—by being an asshole."

"I love you. It wouldn't matter what others say about me."

He laughed, but refused to look her in the eye. "You don't know what love is, sweetheart. If you did, you would see that what happened last night was sex. Good ol' dancing between the sheets."

"That's not true." She stood up and leaned over the table, bracing herself on her hands. "We were friends first, Grayson. We listened to each other, and depended on that friendship to get us through some hard times."

He shrugged. "Your mom left, your dad was struggling to hold his business afloat, and I felt sorry for you."

"Maybe that's true, but even when I grew up you continued to talk with me. You helped me when you didn't need to." She sucked in her breath. "We'd talk about our lives, what kind of car you wanted to buy, and what you planned to do when you stayed in Europe. I was part of your life, Grayson. All that time I was falling deeper in love with you. Can't you see?"

He shook his head. Oh, he could see—perfectly clearly—but he'd never admit it to anyone. "So you had a crush."

"Love. It's called love." She sniffed. "The kind that never goes away or leaves. Trust me, I know. Even when I tried to hate you for ignoring me, for snubbing me in front of your friends, I continued loving you, because…"

His lips thinned. "Because?"

"Because I wasn't going to be like my mom. I wasn't going to stop loving you and disappear from your life the way she did to me, the way your parents did to you. I was going to give us something we've never had. Each other."

The air sizzled with tension. He straightened his shoulders and turned around to hide how much the truth pierced his soul. His parents had shoved him off on his manager when he was fourteen and took most of his income from the tennis tournaments he'd played in to spend their time in Italy, away from their only son. They'd skipped his matches, missed his birthdays. If he was lucky, he got a package delivered at Christmas.

That all ended when the automobile accident had taken their

go-lucky lifestyle away while in Barcelona, and he was left alone. The one person who'd saved him from giving up on everything was Shauna. She'd shown up at the tennis center with a fistful of daisies and forced him to talk about what happened. It was the one time he'd allowed himself to talk about the anger raging inside of him. She was the only reason why he'd never become involved with any other woman on an emotional level. He'd pushed her away, because he knew if he allowed himself to take what she freely offered him, he'd disappoint her…the same way he had his parents.

"You don't know me," he whispered.

She slipped her arms around him from behind and leaned into his back. "I do, and that's why you're scared. I'm scared too, but don't deny what we have together. Don't lie to me."

He swore.

"Let me stay here with you. Today. Tomorrow. I don't care how long. Just don't send me away right now."

He turned around and held her fiercely against him. "Dammit, Shauna. You're too good for me. I'll just hurt you."

"You won't. Never." She held on tight. "Please, let me stay."

"You can stay." Once he spoke the words, he felt ten times lighter. Selfish? Maybe, but he couldn't let her go.

"Really?" She tilted her face up and smiled.

He kissed the tip of her nose. "I can't promise you tomorrow or next week."

"That's enough." She took his hand and pulled him toward the stairs. "Come with me."

He cocked his head. "Where are we going?"

She grinned and wiggled her eyebrows. "I've only got twenty-four hours to convince you to keep me forever and I'm going to start now."

Chapter Twenty-Two

"Grayson!" Shauna covered her bare breasts with her hands and tried to wiggle away from him.

They'd barely left the bed all weekend, and suddenly Grayson grabbed her, saying he wanted to show her something. Not letting her peek, he covered her eyes and led her through a door. Giggles attacked. She was naked, and the breeze tickled her skin.

"You better not be leading me out where everyone can see me. I'll never forgive you." She reached behind her and assured herself that he too was showing his dangling bits to the sky.

A minute later, Grayson stopped walking and slowly removed his hands. She opened her eyes. The late sunlight flickered off the surface of a pool. She dipped her toe in the water and smiled.

"I had no idea you had a pool back here." She gazed around the area of his backyard.

He lowered himself into the water and reached up for her. "No one, besides me and the gardener, comes back here."

"Ever?" She slid in beside him and wrapped her arms around his neck.

Acres of manicured grass, dotted with trees, surrounded the pool area. In the far distance, a practice wall, half hidden by trees, gave her a glimpse into Grayson's life. She kissed his cheek. The thought of him hitting the ball by himself, sequestering himself from others, made her sad.

"Nope. The only people I really bring to the house are my friends, but we always use the pool at the tennis center. The backyard is for me alone. I'm around people every day. This is the one place where I know no one is watching me." He turned around without letting her go. "See the fence? It backs the electric company's property, which is off limits to the public. No one can get to the fence, and the city gave me permission to extend it two feet over the city limit to eight feet tall. They'd have a hard time seeing over."

"I bet you enjoy living here." She smoothed his hair away from his face. "Can I ask you something?"

He nodded.

"Why didn't you keep your parents' house? They had a lovely home."

"When I retired and bought the old rundown tennis center, I originally planned to tear my parents' house down too." He pointed off behind the center. "Instead I combined the two properties. I want to remodel the house and construct a bunker-type lodging where kids can stay during the summer while they're at camp. It's hard for the parents and managers to transport them back and forth, and it's important that they bond with others their own age. The road to being a professional tennis player is a lonely life. In the meantime, I wanted my own place, no memories, just a roof over my head where I could escape. So, I built this one within walking distance to the center and my parents' old place."

"That's a wonderful idea. What's holding you up? Money?" She grabbed onto the wall and let go of him.

He laughed. "No."

She dipped her head back in the water and let her hair fall down her back. "What's so funny?"

"You have no idea how much money I have, do you?" He splashed her.

She scrunched up her nose and wiped her face. "A lot. But you don't compete anymore. All your work is for charity. Don't take this the wrong way, but I know how much you charge for tennis lessons and how much a membership at Schyler's costs…I'm sure you have to plan accordingly."

"Sweetheart, I don't earn money off the tennis center." He pulled her closer, letting her float on the surface of the water. "I still get paid for wearing my sponsors' clothes, being interviewed, doing television shows, and playing in charity events. I keep the center going because that's where my interest lies. I like working with the young kids and motivating them."

"You really are out of my league, aren't you?" She laughed.

"Damn right." He ran his hand over her flat stomach as she lay on the surface. "Around you, I feel like the richest man in the world."

She let her feet drop and tread water. "Why did you retire so young?"

He ignored her question and dove under the water, grabbing her legs. Her scream turned to laughter, and in a matter of seconds, she moaned. She grabbed his hair and pulled him back up.

He shook his head, the water spraying her face. "Let's go in."

"In a minute." She smoothed her hair back. "I've been thinking about my mom, and the fact she's back in my dad's life."

"And?"

"I don't think I can ever forgive her for leaving me." She caught a water droplet off Grayson's cheek. "Does that make me horrible?"

"You?" Grayson shook his head. "I'm the last person who can give you advice on how to deal with parents, but I think that makes you human. Your mom knew the chance of losing you when she left."

"I guess." She sighed. "It's strange how dealing with your parents makes you feel twelve years old again."

Grayson kissed the end of her nose and picked her up. "You feel like a woman to me."

Hand in hand, they headed back to the bedroom, tracking water across the floor on their way. Soon it would be getting dark, and Shauna would have to force herself to go back to the hotel. She had to work tomorrow.

Grayson settled his mouth on hers with a quiet possessiveness.

Carrying her to the bed, he deepened the kiss. His lips tasted slightly salty, and his tongue was soft and sweet. She murmured her approval, her body on continual awareness for how Grayson could make her feel.

"I don't think I'll ever tire of wanting you," he whispered.

The answer to that simmered between them. She pressed closer, rubbed her breasts against him. "Then don't send me away. Let's see if I'm right and we've got what it takes to make this work."

They kissed, sharing light caresses, soothing touches, and bringing each other to a heightened awareness of each other. Her tongue licked across his bottom lip. "Don't deny yourself this."

Each kiss became deeper, more intimate. Their touches grew more heated.

Shauna's heartbeat quickened as Grayson pulled back and cupped her face. "Okay."

"Seriously?" Her chin quivered, afraid to believe.

He gazed pierced her soul. "I promise."

"Forever?" she whispered.

"For as long as we're happy." He kissed her forehead, each eyelid, her nose, before settling on her mouth.

He backed her up to the bed and laid her down. His fingers lingered on her nipples, followed with his mouth. Her skin heated and she arched off the mattress. Her stomach quivered until at last, he entered her. A rush of tiny explosions consumed her and she cried out with pleasure. It was that quick, that sure, that fantastic.

Grayson reached his peak, and his deep moans mixed with hers. When he found his breath, his gravelly voice whispered, "Thank you."

Shauna opened her eyes, unsure what he meant. The look in his eyes explained it all. She placed her hand on his chest, over his heart. "I'll always be here. Forever. No matter what happens between us. I promise."

Chapter Twenty-Three

Shauna made her way along Main Street, or what now was called Grayson Schyler Street, checking the booths that were set up on the sidewalk. Some of the stores had opened early to take advantage of the tourists milling around town before the activities started. The bookstore in particular looked busy and she went in.

Johanna, who ran the daycare, rushed to her side. "Did you see him?"

"Who?" Shauna stood on her tiptoes, but the rows of people blocked her view.

"Bruce Coldwell, that's who." Johanna leaned against her. "I'd give you my house and be your personal assistant for the rest of my life if you introduce me to him."

Shauna laughed, taking in the rosy glow on the young, single mother's cheeks. "I don't know him personally. It would be pretty silly if I walked right up and pushed you into his arms."

Johanna sighed. "Dammit. I thought you brought him to town for my—I mean, the town's benefit."

"That was Grayson's doing. They're good friends," she said.

Johanna's finely arched brows lifted. "You could ask Grayson if he'll let me meet Bruce. From what I hear, he'll do anything for you."

Shauna smiled, knowing she was going to the center in a few minutes to see if she could convince Grayson to meet her tonight. "I'll see what I can do."

"Oh, you are the best." Johanna hugged her. "I've got to get to work before the kids arrive, but I'll be at the tennis center to watch Grayson play against the winner."

"Hey, I'm not promising anything. Grayson and Bruce are busy this week and I'll be lucky if I get a chance to talk with them." She shook her head as Johanna waved off her concern and hurried out the door.

When the crowd remained clustered in the back of the room with no sign of dispersing, Shauna left the store and decided to go to the tennis center. With an extra spring in her step, she dodged the tourists on the sidewalk, biting her lip to keep from laughing with relief. Things were shaping up nicely, and she knew all the hard work she'd put in on organizing the upcoming benefit would pay off for the community.

Sometime during the last three months, she'd forgotten about her goal of proving herself to the town and threw her heart into the fact she was improving lives. She waved to Betty from Mr. Winston's grocery store, and received a thumbs up in reply. Inside, she snickered. It seemed word about her and Grayson being together for the last two weeks circulated the town without any help from her. More surprising, the community seemed to support her. She hoped the next few days during the benefit would put her back on solid ground as an upstanding citizen in Cottage Grove.

"Shauna!" From down the sidewalk, Grayson flagged her down.

He threw his arm over a beautiful woman at his side with a familiarity that caused Shauna to stop in her tracks. She closed her mouth. The pictures of Crista in the magazines didn't compare to her in real life.

With powerful long legs and a graceful walk, Crista turned heads as she strolled with Grayson toward Shauna. Shauna envied the natural openness of the woman's smile and the short, sassy hairstyle with a hint of pink highlights on her bangs.

"Shauna, I'd like you to meet Crista Johnson." He moved over to Shauna's side. "Crista, this is Shauna Marino, she's the one running the event and your go-to gal if you need anything."

Shauna smiled through her confusion of why Grayson wouldn't announce her as his girlfriend, and shook it off as being petty. This was business, and she was a professional.

"Welcome to Cottage Grove, Ms. Johnson." She shook Crista's hand. "Thank you so much for helping out."

"Please, call me Crista." She laid her hand on Grayson's shoulder. "Grayson has filled me in on all you've done in such a short time, and I can't help but admire your drive and ambition for your town. Coming from a larger city, it's refreshing to hear how tight of a community you all have here. Grayson has shared some of the history with me, I'm enthralled."

Shauna wanted to hate her. She really did. Crista's sultry southern accent, along with her seductive grace, had her feeling inadequate and small, but her candidness and smile put a Band-Aid on her insecurities to see the wonderful person she'd read about in all her research.

Grayson slipped his hand into Shauna's and she glanced at him before saying to Crista, "I can't thank you enough for donating your time. Has Grayson showed you where you'll be staying?"

Crista pressed her hand on her stomach. "We were headed over there now. I convinced him to come along and eat breakfast with me at the hotel. Why don't you join us?"

"Oh, I would like that, but I'm afraid I need to go meet the others who are coming." She reached out and caught Crista's arm. "But I'd love to talk with you more before the activities start. How about I buy you dinner tonight?"

"Better yet, why don't you come over to the house, Crista? Dominic and Gary are staying with me, you remember them, and you can meet the others who are due in this afternoon." Grayson glanced between her and Christa before settling his gaze on Shauna. "I'll call the hotel and see if they have time to cater dinner. Will you have everything wrapped up by seven tonight?"

She nodded. "Sounds great.

Grayson kissed her. "Thanks, sweetheart. I'll see you later then. I better go feed Crista before she knocks me down."

She snorted. "Be nice. I want to get to know her better. I have a ton of questions I'm dying to ask. Besides, I can tell she's too sweet to hurt anyone."

"No, I'm not." Crista laughed. "You'll have to ask him what happened when he said I couldn't beat him in golf because I'm a girl."

"Oh, no you didn't." Shauna laughed and slapped at Grayson's shoulder. "I hope she kicked your butt."

"She annihilated me, and then forced me speak to the whole crowd about the power of women in sports." Grayson shook his head, but his smile came easily. "I'll never be able to step foot in that city again."

She joined the laughter. "Okay, you two get going. I don't want Crista harming you. I sorta like you just the way you are."

Crista stepped over and hugged her, whispering in her ear. "I take it you're the one who's put the smile on Grayson's face. We'll definitely talk tonight."

"I can't wait," Shauna replied, and watched them walk away.

Her earlier assessment of Crista had been wrong. She was Grayson's friend, nothing else, and Shauna couldn't help but like her. She smiled. Even though she had wondered if Crista and Grayson were together in the past, Grayson had made it clear he and Crista were only good friends.

Running late, she hurried to her car and headed out to the tennis center to meet the others. Ten minutes later, she stood inside the lobby surrounded by the biggest, most intimidating men she'd ever seen. At a loss for words, she stared up into the face of Gary Satchel, defensive lineman for the Pittsburgh Steelers.

If Crista's big personality had her feeling small, Gary's six-foot-four frame and gazillion pounds of muscles reduced her to a breadcrumb. His dark brown eyes creased at the corners as he leaned down and wrapped his mammoth arms around her. She held her breath, prepared to have her ribs cracked, but he gently squeezed before letting her go.

"So, you're Shauna, Grayson's stalker." Gary stepped back and seemed to admire her body. "I don't know how many times I've wanted to fly over and shake your hand for keeping Grayson on his toes."

"Me?" She laid her hand on her chest. "Whatever he's told you was fabricated."

"I hope not." Gary laughed. "I'd be disappointed to hear that a woman with that much spunk didn't exist. Is it true you spray painted his name over and over on the road for five miles on the way out of town years ago?"

"Um. Well, some of it might be true. I thought the message would show how much we all loved him here in Cottage Grove as he drove to the airport." She grinned. "Let's just say I've grown up and no longer do things like that. Maybe you can pretend I'm a well-mannered professional that's grateful to you for helping with the benefit instead."

"But you'll tell more stories about how you drove Grayson crazy later?" His brows rose in hope.

She leaned in and whispered, "Deal."

The next man shouldered Gary out of the way and stuck his hand out to her. "I'm Dominic Chekovsky. You can call me Dominic and I will call you beautiful."

She laughed at the very precise way Dominic talked. "I think I'm going to have to watch you. You'll have half the women in town ready to move out of the area to follow you wherever you go."

He nodded, his mouth thinning the longer it took him to answer. "It happens. It is not something I can help."

Despite his big ego, Dominic's baby face, including a gapped toothed grin, had her instantly liking the man. He totally blew her image of the stereotypical beat-up hockey player with his blond good looks and soft-spoken voice. She could understand why the magazines have dubbed him a Russian magnet.

"Okay, this is what I've got for you both." She passed them each a folder. "I'll need you to—"

"Wait." Dominic removed the rest of the papers out of her hands, and slipped her hand under his elbow. "Business later. Lunch now."

Before she could protest, Dominic and Gary had her sitting in the driver's spot of her car. She gazed over at Gary sandwiched sideways in the backseat of her little hatchback. Dominic sat in the front, his knees squeezed against the dashboard, and she laughed.

"Okay, guys, what do you feel like eating?"

"Steak." Their voices blended into one.

She shook her head, amused. "All right, guys, steak it is."

"So, Shauna." Dominic pushed back from the dashboard. "What's your plan?"

"My plan?" She glanced over at him and raised her brows. "What do you mean?"

"How do you plan on winning Grayson? He's got a lot of girlfriends." Dominic ducked away from Gary's punch. "Maybe I can help you."

"Damn, Dominic. Lay off her," Gary muttered.

Girlfriends? She pushed down on the accelerated and squeezed the steering wheel. Next time she had a few minutes alone with Grayson, she would find out about his *girlfriends*.

Chapter Twenty-Four

Shauna reluctantly excused herself, and stepped out of Grayson's front door. Her skin tingled from the rush of warm night air compared to the chill from the inside air conditioning. She'd expected to feel awkward around Grayson's friends, and instead found herself joining in on the teasing and stories.

Grayson and his friends had history together, and a common bond. Each of them understood the highs and lows of being in the public eye, and seemed to enjoy their time together where they could relax and visit. She soon found out that they teased Grayson unmercifully about all the women after him and she was able to relax, knowing Dominic's earlier comment was part of that teasing.

She sat down on the step, planted her elbows on her knees, and propped her chin in her hands. Grayson had surprised her by barely leaving her side all evening. Contentment washed through her. If he wasn't holding her hand, he was pulling her onto his lap, sneaking kisses, and letting everyone see how they felt toward each other. He'd come full circle and seemed to be over his reluctance to have a relationship.

And, once the benefit was over, she'd take her dad out to dinner and ask him if he'd like to go apartment hunting with her. The realtor she'd called had sent a printout of houses available, but most were too far out of the city or not in her price range. It looked more promising to rent for the time being. Maybe having her dad involved in the search would put her life back on even ground, and she could make things right with him again.

The door opened behind her, and she glanced over her shoulder. She smiled and patted the spot beside her. Grayson sat down, and she leaned her head on his shoulder.

"Hey, you." She wrapped her arms around his waist. "Shouldn't you be entertaining your friends?"

"They're fine on their own." He kissed the top of her head. "Are you okay?"

She nodded. "Perfect. I came out to wrap my head around what all is involved with the events tomorrow. Do you think I've covered any problems that'll arise? I haven't even seen the media yet. What if they don't show up? They probably think Cottage Grove's small news and not worth their time."

"They'll come." He stretched his legs out. "Earlier, at the hotel, Stan Dogger was singing your praises to all the customers, and telling them how he always knew you were an important part of why Cottage Grove is special."

"He's such a nice man." She smiled. "I think he was ready to retire from his position at the Chamber of Commerce. Did you know he's a great grandpa now? Jason's wife had a little girl a few days ago."

"He's a good man. I remember how he stepped up and helped me handle the paperwork on the house when my parents died." Grayson sighed. "What do you say about staying over tonight and keeping me company?"

"Company, huh?" She laughed. "I shouldn't. You've got guests, and I need to start work early to set up everything Dominic will need at the park."

"I was hoping we could have this time together. I promised Crista I'd run the time clock for the race tomorrow, so I'll probably only get to see you between events," he said.

She pouted. "Poor baby. I'll have to make it up to you in three days when this is all over."

Grayson growled and nuzzled her neck. "You better."

"I will." She wiggled away from him, laughing. "I promise."

"It's already dark. Let me run in and grab my keys. I'll drive you back to the hotel." He stood up.

She stopped him. "I'll walk. The streetlights emit enough light for me to see my way. I'm so wound up about doing everything perfect this week that a nice walk will relax me. I'll sleep like a baby tonight."

Grayson grinned, held up his finger for her not to move before glancing behind him. He turned back around and grabbed her hand, tugging her off the porch and into the garage. She watched him with amusement as he lowered the garage doors casting them into darkness, and laughed as he ran into one of his cars and grunted in pain, finding his way back to her side.

"So much for being dashing and sexy." He opened the car door and helped her into the backseat.

"You gain points on spontaneity." She laughed. "I hope you're not in too much pain."

He groaned. "I know for a fact there's no feeling in my knee. All the blood has rushed north. I hope you're taking off your clothes…"

She was already ahead of him. Her shirt was off, and she grabbed for his, dragging it over his head. Within seconds, she'd flung her shorts in the front seat and lay underneath him. His erection nudged at the slick wetness between her legs.

"Oh God…we need a condom." She fumbled in the dark, trying to sit up.

"Got one." He chuckled as he kneeled between her legs. "If I couldn't convince you to stay, I was going to sneak into the hotel later tonight after everyone else was asleep, so I put one in my pocket."

"Only one?" She giggled.

"Better watch it, sweetheart. I might take that as an invitation and pay you a middle of the night visit." His hands roamed over her body, finding her breasts.

"Promise?"

He growled.

She wrapped her legs around his waist and thrust her hips forward in invitation. He never hesitated, but slid inside her in one long, wet glide. Shauna whimpered at how perfectly they fit together. Hot and hard, he filled her.

She quivered with tension. The need to have him move inside her left her breathless. But he remained still, buried to the hilt. He kissed her, his tongue teasing hers, his lips urging, demanding, caressing, while his arms tightly flexed. It was too much. She had to move.

He broke the kiss, using his elbows to take his weight as he pulled out of her, leaving the head of his hardness inside.

"God, Grayson. More."

Only then did he start to move, setting up a slow, steady rhythm, letting her join him in finding her pleasure. She got lost in the heat of the moment. Each thrust and withdrawal of his body causing delicious friction between them, she couldn't slow down.

It took no time for the fire to build. She clawed at Grayson's back, making soft noises as her body grew tense. He lowered his head and pulled her nipple into his mouth. His hand slid between their bodies and found the spot that'd send her over the edge.

She stiffened as his thumb brushed over her. Her body squeezed around him. Then he stroked her again and she exploded, moaning his name, her body melting under him.

He murmured his pleasure near her ear, letting her ride out her orgasm, draining the last shudder from her. Then, when she was satisfied, he allowed himself to lose control. His thrusts became wilder, stronger, and more urgent. She stroked his chest, moving under him, encouraging him. He plunged deeply one last time and laid his forehead on hers, his breath coming out in a heated rush as he climaxed.

He was dead weight on her as he seemed to struggle to gain strength to remove himself from her body. When he finally stirred and started to push himself off, she stopped him.

"Not yet," she said.

He pressed his pelvis back between her legs, and braced himself on his elbows, smoothing the hair off her face. "I'm too heavy."

"You're perfect." She smiled into the darkness. "I want to ask you something."

"Sure." He stifled a yawn.

"Is everything okay? I mean, between us?"

He kissed her forehead, and hauled himself off her. "Yeah. Why?"

"I don't know." She sat up. "Maybe it's the stress of hosting the event that's getting to me. I just wanted to make sure."

Chapter Twenty-Five

Friday morning seemed to arrive the minute after Shauna placed her head on her pillow. After staying too late at Grayson's house the night before, she'd set her alarm clock for an hour earlier than normal and arrived in the park as the maintenance crew finished roping the area off.

Long tables lined the closest side of the field where she'd scheduled Dominic to perform during the day. There were trash bins, portable outhouses, and enough signs erected to direct the people on where to line up for the activities, and keep chaos from taking over. She spotted Dominic standing with a group of men all dressed in black near midfield. She bit her lip to keep from laughing. He'd told her he'd come with his own security team, but seriously? Suited men with darkened sunglasses? In Cottage Grove? *Yeah, nobody will notice them.*

"There you are, beautiful." Dominic stepped around the table, leaned down, and kissed Shauna's cheek. "I want you to make sure the children are placed first in line. We must keep their safety our top priority."

"O...kay." She raised her brows. "Although, I imagine kids will be coming throughout the day, because it's Teacher In-Service Day, and there's no school."

"It doesn't matter. It's the women." He nodded, and gave her an indulgent smile as if she was slow on the uptake. "You'll see."

"I know we've only known each other less than twenty-four hours, Dominic, but really? Give us women a little respect. Not everyone is going to turn into a nymphomaniac today. This is a public area and females do have self-respect. Look at me. I'm able to hold myself back from stripping my clothes off and jumping you right here." She laughed, but her amusement cut short at noticing the seriousness etched on Dominic's face. "You know what I mean."

He straightened and gazed down his broad nose at her. "I do not understand. There must be something wrong with you. All women find me attractive. This is not natural."

"Normal or not, you wouldn't want me. Trust me." She patted his arm. "Let's walk over to the field, and you can see how you'll be making shots with a hockey stick and a rubber ball. I'm sorry about not having an ice rink at your disposal, but this was the closest I could come up with in such a short time."

"It is fine." He approached the stack of hockey sticks, grinned, and struck a pose. "I look good, yes?"

She rolled her eyes. "I've seen better."

"You tease." He winked before putting the equipment away.

Dominic's entourage surrounded him on all sides, their arms folded, their faces void of emotion.

She tilted her head and studied the one closest to her. "Um, Dominic?"

"Yes, beautiful?"

"Are they wearing some kind of listening devices?" She stared at the almost transparent wire that traveled from the inside of the guard's ear, down his neck, and disappeared inside the collar of his black suit.

"Yes." Dominic lifted his leg, pulled up his jeans, and displayed a small box strapped to his muscled calf. "Along with being able to hear me wherever I go, I'm also implanted with a tracking device."

"Shit." She stared in horror. "Is that in case you run off and someone turns you in at the dog pound?"

"I do not understand what this pound place you talk about is but yes, if I am kidnapped, they will find me." He shrugged. "Don't worry though. We've only had that happen once."

She blinked several times. "This is so bizarre."

Loud voices reached them. She turned, but before she could say anything, Dominic's x-team picked her up and set her to the side out of the way, and then took up their positions around Dominic. She huffed, a little put out with their rude behavior.

Everything happened faster than she could react. Women— more women than she ever thought she'd see in Cottage Grove— rushed the field. Mothers left children unattended, yards away in strollers. Older children turned in a circle, searching for their mothers, lost. She scanned the mob. There were women screaming, crying, and pushing and—oh my God, did that woman faint?

Shauna turned around and sought Dominic. Safely tucked behind the wall of bodyguards, he appeared seemingly unperturbed about the fanfare. He shrugged his large shoulders and mouthed *I told you.*

The security team held the women back, but they couldn't keep it up for long. They were severely outnumbered. Where had all the women come from?

She'd have to act fast. A catastrophe was the last thing she needed on the opening day of the event.

Shauna jogged over to the picnic table and climbed on the top. "Can I have your attention?" She cleared her throat. "Excuse me!"

No one paid her any mind. They dedicated their pursuit to push and jump and scream in their need to get closer to Dominic. She stuck her fingers in her mouth and sent a deafening whistle over the crowd of females. They froze and turned to her without uttering a sound.

"Dominic is willing to challenge everyone, one at a time, to try and get a goal past him." She inhaled deeply. "That means every single woman, I mean person, will have his whole attention, but to do that you'll have to listen. Dominic has requested that children go first."

The ladies groaned. She held out her hands and motioned for them to calm down. She'd never seen mass hysteria at this level over one male in her life.

"If you all will line up, we can start organizing the event. Remember, its two dollars for one shot. The more money you spend, the more tries you'll get." She caught a group of women sneaking in front of the kids. "Children first!"

Fifteen minutes later, she breathed a sigh of relief. The games had begun, and the women watched quietly, if not stubbornly, from their place in line. The cash box overflowed with money, already exceeding her projected goal. With more people heading toward the field, she walked toward her car to grab another container when she saw Diana.

"Look at this crowd. Where did they all come from?" Diana gazed past Shauna.

She hitched her thumb over her shoulder. "Dominic Chekovsky, professional hockey player, and apparently a babe magnet of mega proportions."

Diana groaned. "Ugh. Muscles wasted on the dumb."

"Do me a favor. Will you help the others keep control of the group? I need to find something else to hold all the money that's coming in on this event. Those women are not going to stop paying until Dominic calls an end to his day. It's insane. There are even women who I know are married making fools of themselves over him."

"Sure." She smiled. "It'll give me time to check out the eye candy, and make fun of our friends."

Shauna grinned. "Enjoy."

On the way to the parking lot, she dug her phone out of her jeans and checked her messages in case Grayson had called. Nothing.

Not surprising, because Grayson had promised to help Bruce set up the trout pond at the lake and it was still early. An inflatable three-foot swimming pool stocked with fish from the closest hatchery would provide a guaranteed catch for the kids twelve years old and under. Bruce would divide his time between motivating the children and handing out fly-fishing tips to the adults.

Shauna threw herself into keeping chaos from happening around Dominic and the rest of the day flashed by her in a blur. She'd missed lunch and dinner, and still Dominic continued to challenge the community. Her pockets bulged from the amount of money Dominic brought in, and she could only hope that the other athletes would do so well.

A familiar laugh brought her gaze up and she smiled. Her dad stepped out on the field with a hockey stick in his hand. She stood up, moved to the front of the crowd, and whistled, happy he took time off from fixing cars to have a little fun.

"Come on, Dad. You can win!" She clapped.

Dominic raised his brows. "Oh, beautiful, you wound me. I always win."

She laughed. "You're going down. That's my dad, and he's the best."

As Dominic lined up to shoot the ball into the goal, Tony turned around, smiled, and sent a wink toward the crowd. Shauna followed his line of vision and found her mom clapping on the sidelines a few yards away from her. She scowled. The thought of her dad enjoying the day with someone else, particularly the woman who'd left her own family, left her nauseous.

When was the last time she'd convinced her dad to take time off and go out to dinner with her or see a movie? She swallowed hard. Her new job took so much of her time, she'd put off connecting with him since she got back home. *Shit. I'm the worst daughter.*

She studied her mother. While she'd been gone, the years hadn't been kind to her. The soft, young face Shauna remembered was replaced with lined wrinkles around tired eyes and a thinner mouth. She'd cut her long black hair short, and there were gray streaks through her bangs. The smile—she glanced away—was the same.

Not able to face how disconnected she felt around her family, she took her box to another worker to oversee, and made her excuses. She hurried through the park to her car. In the safety of her vehicle, away from the memories, she called Grayson. He picked up on the first ring.

"Hey, you." She let her head fall back on the seat. "I'm so glad you answered."

"Is everything okay?"

"Yeah." She swallowed. "I'm starving, and thought I'd stop and pick up a pizza. What do you think about having me deliver it to your house? I won't even ask you to tip me."

"Sounds delicious."

She smiled. "Great. I'll be there in a little bit."

Chapter Twenty-Six

"Oh." Shauna groaned loud and long. "Yes!"

Grayson moved lower. "Right here?"

"Mm hm." She waited, braced for the pressure, and clawed at the floor as Grayson lunged against her. "That. Feels. So. G-good."

The door slammed. Grayson never stopped. She turned her head to see who came in and groaned out in pleasure.

"Hey, Dominic. How did the—" She moaned, and waited until Grayson finished messaging her back and moved off of her. "How did your event go?"

"The women are insane. They are still there. I can't get rid of them." Dominic rubbed the back of his neck. "I'm afraid they won't leave the park. It took my security team a half hour driving down a lot of roads before they could sneak me back here without any of them following us."

She clicked her tongue and stood up. "Poor baby. Come here and lie down on the floor. My back is killing me. I can only imagine how you're feeling after facing so many challenges all day long."

Dominic stepped over and lay down on his stomach. Shauna reached for Grayson's hands for leverage, and then stepped barefooted onto Dominic's broad back. He groaned, and she grinned at Grayson. "We could go into business together. You could do messages, and I could take my frustrations out on people by stomping on them. Tell me again why we're busting our asses making money for Cottage Grove?"

"It's our home." Grayson leaned over and kissed her.

"This is good." Dominic closed his eyes. "Are you sure you're not fantasizing about me? You don't have a foot fetish, do you?"

"Nope." She laughed. "I might as well be your sister for how much I'm not attracted to you."

"Strange," Dominic muttered. "I think something is wrong with your woman, Grayson."

She dug her toes into Dominic's ribs. "Hey. Watch it. You're not in the position to make insults."

"You're hurting his feelings." Grayson laughed.

A few minutes later, soft snores floated in the room and Shauna gently stepped off Dominic's back. She motioned Grayson to follow her. In the kitchen, she put the extra food left over from dinner in the fridge.

"Make sure you wake him up in a little bit and send him to bed. Dominic worked harder than I ever expected. He deserves a full night's sleep." She closed the fridge. "Is it always like that for him? The women, I mean…they're savages around him. They treated him as if he's some sex slave come to earth to please them. Some of their comments made me want to slap them. I can't imagine how he keeps his cool. They have no idea what a nice man he is. They only see him for a sexy jock, and that's wrong. I don't think he enjoys all the women's attention."

"That's why he was hiding out in his home country of Russia. He's told me before that back there, the women ignore him and he can live normally. Staying in the States is hell for him. He can't escape from the fanatics." Grayson leaned against the counter. "No one really understands what makes women go crazy around him. He's had a company hound him for the last couple of years, because they want to bottle his sweat. They believe he emits more pheromones than the average man."

She wrinkled her nose. "That's gross."

"That's what Dominic says." Grayson pulled her over to him and looped his arms around her waist. "So tell me, do you really feel nothing around him?"

"Of course not." She cupped his face, running her thumb over the slight indention on his chin. "It's all about you. You make me squeal and do silly things to get your attention. No one has ever come close to making me work as hard as you to gain your attention. That must make you worth all the trouble, huh?"

"Yeah, you do have a way about you that makes me pay attention." He grinned.

She nodded. "I swear, next week I'll go back to my normal stalker-like self. I'll drive you nuts."

He kissed her softly. "I miss having you all to myself. I can't wait until the charity event is over and our lives go back to normal. I want you in my bed every night."

She pressed against his chest. "Only your bed? Wow, you know how to sweet talk a lady, don't you?"

"You know what I mean. I miss you." He laid her head in the nook between his neck and shoulder. "I've been a fool when it comes to you, and have a lot to make up for when my friends leave."

"That sounds perfect." She closed her eyes and let him hold her. "You won't find any argument from me."

"Figured not." He chuckled.

"I hate to go, but I'll never make it through the rest of the events that are planned if I don't head home, soak in the tub, and get some sleep." She opened her eyes and leaned back. "You better rest up, the press is landing tomorrow, and you still have to play against the winners of the tournament on Sunday. I heard you have a couple of players you trained yourself gunning for you."

"Yeah, they talk big but have never seen me play full out in person before." He kissed her once more, and tucked her hair behind her ear. "I'll see you out."

Hand in hand, they walked back through the house, stepped over Dominic who was still out cold on the living room floor, and went out the front door. She gazed up at the sky. The stars twinkled in the sky.

"I hope it doesn't get too hot tomorrow. Bruce will be okay at the lake, but Crista has three runs she promised to do. Juan's taken the high school gym. I figured that was the easiest place for him to show off his ski line, and sign autographs." She slapped her forehead. "I forgot to let Gary know we switched him from the field at the school to the park. The maintenance crew thought it would be less hassle to leave everything set up from Dominic's event and use it for Gary."

"Don't worry. I'll let him know," Grayson said.

"I think I need a drink." She stopped at her car and wrapped her arms around his waist. "Let's get drunk when this is all over."

"That'll take two drinks." He tickled her side. "You're a lightweight."

"Gah. Don't remind me." She kissed him.

"I'm worried about you. What you've done is a huge undertaking." He ran his fingers through her hair. "With your mom back, you haven't had any time to yourself. You're going to have to face your family when all this is over. The stress isn't good for you."

"I know." She licked her bottom lip. "I miss my dad one minute, and then the next second I'm so mad."

"At your mom?"

She nodded. "Dad, too. How can he let her come waltzing back into his life? It's like he's forgotten everything we went through after she left."

Grayson opened his mouth, hesitated, and closed his jaw. She frowned.

"What were you going to say?" She waited.

"Maybe there's more to the story. You were young when she left." He tilted her chin up. "It probably wouldn't hurt to talk with her. Get everything out in the open."

"If you had the chance to talk to your parents again, to confront them for leaving you all alone, would you?"

His mouth tightened.

"Never mind." She smoothed out the lines on his face with her hands. "That's two separate problems, and I shouldn't have asked."

He kissed her forehead. "Just think about what I said. If you decide to talk with them, I'll be here for you, okay?"

"Thanks." She ducked her chin. "Right now, I want to ignore the fact that she's pushed herself back in my life. It was easier when she was gone. I'll keep myself busy, and when this is all over, I'll have a talk with my dad. We'll figure it out. We always do."

He cupped the back of her neck and held her in place, while he took the kiss deeper. Her eyes closed and her legs shook as she melted under his touch. If she didn't leave now, she'd talk herself into staying and both of them would suffer tomorrow when they were dragging themselves around to the events.

She pulled away at the same time a bright flash lit up the driveway, blinding her. Grayson threw his arm around her shoulders and tucked her against his chest as he hurried to open the car door. She continued to blink away the dots clouding her vision.

"Dammit. It's the press. Get inside and drive away." He put his hand on the top of her head and pushed her into the car. "Take the back roads into town, and make sure they don't follow you to the hotel before you get out of the car. I'll do my best to hold them here, and give you a head start. Go. Go!"

She nodded. Her hands shook as she tried to start her car. She threw the gear in reverse, but there were two cameramen blocking her exit. She peered out at Grayson, not knowing what to do. He motioned her to go the other direction through the front lawn.

Without thinking, and still struggling to see past the spots floating in front of her from the flash, she pressed the accelerator, shot forward, and left burn marks in Grayson's perfectly manicured lawn.

Chapter Twenty-Seven

Grayson kept his hands down at his sides, and watched Shauna tear out of his driveway. His breath lodged in his chest, and he forced himself to face the reporters.

"Grayson, who's the woman you were kissing?" A tall man shoved a microphone in front of his face. "Is she someone from your past?"

Another man, shorter this time, held up a bright light. "Give us some background on your new love interest. Did you kick her out before the night was over? What happened to the last blond-haired woman you were seeing? Jessica? Is it true you dumped her for a supermodel?"

Grayson reached into his pocket and held up his phone. "You're on private property, and I'll give you two minutes to get back in your van and leave."

"What's her name?" The man remained standing in front of him.

He pushed a button and glared at them. "Clock's ticking, boys."

"Rumors are going around that she's your mistress, and you've kept her hidden away for years. Is that true? Do you have plans to make this a permanent relationship?"

"I'm not answering any questions. On Sunday, you're all invited to the tournament and the final event. I will answer any question about my professional life there, but my personal life is off limits. Tomorrow, you'll concentrate on the other athletes and do whatever needs to be done to support Cottage Grove. That's why you're here. Do you understand?" He stepped toward them, backing them up.

"Sure, sure. Give us the woman's name, and we won't mention it until after the event." The tall man motioned for the camera crew. "Get a close up. Let's show the television viewers how we've caught the golden boy in the middle of having a private affair."

"That's it. I'm calling the police." He turned his back, punched the button for his own voice mail, and walked to the house. "Yes, this is Grayson Schyler at—"

Shouting commenced. He glanced behind him. The car doors slammed and the van engine revved. He shook his head in disgust. "Assholes."

He walked into the house, locked the door, and set the security alarm. After waking Dominic up and telling him to go to bed, he climbed the stairs to his room. The dinner he'd eaten earlier churned in his stomach and he popped a couple antacids from the nightstand in his mouth before moving over to the window.

The press had cleared out from the front of his house, and he leaned his forehead against the glass. The relief he should've felt refused to come. His chest tightened, and he squeezed his eyes shut. He couldn't let them put Shauna through the hell they were capable of or make her doubt their relationship. It'd destroy her.

Too sweet and gentle, she'd fall apart under the pressure. They'd insinuate that he was using her, and belittle what they shared.

Going to college was supposed to have been her one-way ticket away from him and the life that would've crumbled her love for him after time. She'd been too young, and he'd only wanted to keep her happy. He'd wanted her to achieve everything she deserved.

He'd never expected her to return, acting as if nothing had changed between them. He closed his eyes briefly. He'd gone from believing he'd lost her for six years to finally having her back in his life, and he wasn't willing to let the damn reporters take that away from him.

The amount of shit that came with being in the public eye had ruined many people. He'd seen it himself. And he saw the fear and apprehension when they peppered Shauna with questions. This was his life, not hers.

He ran his hands through his hair. Shauna and her damn good deeds. No one cared about her fixing all her past mistakes. She couldn't see that everyone in town loved her for who she was, that they could see past the childhood choices she made, no matter how destroying they'd been. She was Shauna, who loved deeper, cared stronger, and tried harder than anyone he knew.

She should never have planned the fundraiser. The reporters and news cameras would expect her to spend time in front of the lens, and Grayson would be useless to stop them from putting doubt in her mind.

He moved away from the window and dragged his feet into the bathroom to start the shower. He had no idea how to fix everything, but he was damn sure he'd do whatever it took to make sure she felt exonerated. She wanted others to view her as the mature, responsible woman that she was, and he'd bulldoze anyone down who tried to take that away from her.

If that included keeping the press away or punching anyone who got close to her, he'd do it. He'd seen what reporters could do to a person.

Shauna lived a sheltered lifestyle. There was no safe place for love when everyone wanted the dirt, the scandal, the mistakes. Fame had destroyed his parents and had sucked him dry while playing the circuit—he wouldn't allow that to happen to Shauna.

For the first time, he damned their age difference. If he'd only known her before he'd become famous. If he'd experienced what it was like to love Shauna back then, he would've done anything to keep her. Instead, he'd let her go because he had a career, and now he was going to have to figure out a way to make her understand there was no going back. He was a former Wimbledon champ, and the press would always be around.

He removed his phone from his pocket, and pushed the button. He'd call her and make sure she arrived back at the hotel without any problems. Then he'd figure out a way for them to get together, away from the press, and hopefully he'd keep her safe until the benefit was over.

Shauna's voice mail came on. He cussed. "Hey. Call me. Please."

He waited, needing to say more and coming up empty. How was he supposed to tell her he loved her when he couldn't see her face, her eyes?

Hanging up, he threw the phone on the dresser.

He had no idea if the reporters would find out where Shauna was staying. She was open and trusting. They'd have her confessing on tape. They'd take her love and turn it into something wrong and ugly.

She'd grow to hate him, and the thought of her regretting every second they were together wounded him. If she weren't depending on making a success of the event, he'd almost be tempted to fly her out of the country tonight. They could hide away in the Bahamas, or go to Cancun.

He stubbed his toe on the bathroom doorframe. "God dammit!"

In his pain, he threw himself at the door, slamming his shoulder against the wood. The splurge of energy did nothing but feed his anger.

Shauna always affected him in the worst way. He became weak and selfish around her. His common sense fled for the chance to make her smile.

Forgetting about the shower, he slid on a pair of shorts, put his sneakers on, and hurried downstairs. He grabbed the center's keys off the front table, and ran across the lawn.

He walked through the lobby in the dark. After grabbing a racket from behind the counter, he flicked on the first court lights and headed out on the playing area. The fluorescent bulbs flickered, trying to power up to their full capacity. He was in no mood to wait, and loaded the ball machine.

He flipped the switch, ran to the other side, and lunged for the first ball. Bouncing on the balls of his feet, he hit forehands, one after another, drilling the balls over the net and pinging off the curtain. Each swing left him grunting, throwing all his strength into beating his opponent.

After a few minutes, he fell into a routine. Each ball represented a threat to Shauna, and he smashed it over to the other side of the court with all his power. Sweat dripped down into his eyes, but he kept going. He couldn't stop.

The machine took two hundred tennis balls, and he returned them faster, harder each time, letting himself sink back into a routine that was more familiar to him than waking up every morning. This is where he belonged. This was what he could control.

Out on the court, he could pretend his life was easy, that there wasn't a woman loving him, and pain ready to take someone he loved. He was playing a game. One he knew well.

Repetitive movements, constant power, and two hundred tennis balls later, he dropped his racket on the court and walked out. He walked down the hallway to his office. Leaving the lights off, he sunk down in his chair, and buried his head in his hands.

He knew what he had to do.

"I'm not letting you go this time, sweetheart." He ground the heels of his palms into his eyes. "You're mine. You've always been mine."

Chapter Twenty-Eight

"Juan!" Shauna jogged across the school parking lot until she reached his side. "Have you seen Grayson? I can't find him anywhere."

"No." He flipped his shaggy blond hair to the side. "Now that you mention it, he wasn't at the house when I left either."

She bit her bottom lip. Something was wrong. He was supposed to meet her at the park and take the press around to the different sites where the celebrities were working. Instead, the park was empty of cameras and she couldn't find Grayson anywhere.

"If he shows up, can you ask him to call me?" She brushed the wrinkles out of his shirtsleeve. "Yeesh, Juan, it looks like you live in a suitcase."

"Hey. It's the look I'm going for." He beamed at her with the straightest teeth she'd ever seen. "The chicks love it."

"Hm. I bet they do." She sighed. "Anyway, I'll be out at the lake this morning helping Bruce. Tell Grayson to call me. It's important."

"No problemo." He lifted the strap of his duffle bag with his good arm, and headed toward the gym. "Thanks for sending over all my supplies. Not being able to use my shoulder makes my life complex. It sucks. I can't wait 'til they give me the okay to start acting like a human again."

She studied the way the elastic strap held his wrist to his ribs, immobilizing his shoulder. "How much longer do you have to take it easy?"

"Coach says two weeks, but I'm hoping to talk the doctor into letting me start therapy next week." He grinned. "The doc wants me to date her sister, so I think I can work something out with her."

She laughed. "Don't push yourself. You've gained a fan, and I want to see you on the slopes soon."

"Dump Grayson and we can scoot to the mountain right now and get a run on." He winked. "There's nothing like snuggling to keep warm."

She shook her head. "Not on your life. Not even for you."

"Good answer. Grayson's a lucky man. I'm happy for you two," he said.

Shauna left Juan laughing, and strolled to her car. She drove the shortcut through her old neighborhood, glancing at her dad's house and the garage, before taking her foot off the gas pedal and stopping along the curb. *Oh my God.*

The freshly mowed lawn, the flowerpots decorating the porch, and the flag blowing in the wind gave her a glimpse of how much her dad's life had changed since her mother had come back. He'd begun to take pride in his home again. Her hands slipped off the steering wheel. Even the shutters around the kitchen window now matched the rest of the house.

What would cause a grown man to remain faithful to his wife after all the years spent asking questions to the air and feeing abandoned? She slouched in the seat. Belinda had never called, sent a letter, or checked up on her family. If her mother loved her dad so much, how could she do that?

What kind of mother leaves her daughter without any regrets? She thumped her hand against the steering wheel. She swore never do that to someone she loved.

Tony stepped out of the garage and lifted his arm in the air. Shauna waved back. She should go, but instead she found herself opening the door and walking down the driveway.

"I figured you were busy today. Everyone is talking about all the stars, and the events planned. You've done a real good job making something of Cottage Grove, sweetheart." Tony ruffled her hair when he hugged her, making her smile.

Some things never changed.

Some things she never wanted to change.

Her dad's love was one of them, and she knew whatever hold her mom had on him, if she was going to continue her relationship with her dad, she'd have to deal with the whole package. She just wasn't ready to lower her armor and allow herself to get hurt again.

"I am, but not too busy to stop and see my dad." She gazed over at the house. "I'm on my way over to the lake now. You should come on over and learn something from Bruce. Might help you catch more fish."

Tony smiled. "Half the fun of fishing was the company I kept. We had some good times drowning worms, huh?"

She nodded. "Some of the best memories I have."

"Mine too," he said.

She glanced everywhere but at him. "The house looks nice. You cut the grass."

"Yeah." He pointed to the porch. "Belinda's been planting things in all those empty pots I had in the garage, and even has more flowers in back still in the flats. She wants me to make window boxes next. I told her before long it'll look like an old couple lives here and she'll want me to paint the house yellow."

She shuffled her feet. "I better go. It was good seeing you, Dad. Maybe next week we can go out to dinner. Just the two of us. I have something to tell you."

"Oh, yeah?" He smiled. "Good news, I hope."

"The very best." She grinned.

"Is this about Grayson?" He adjusted his baseball cap. "I've heard the rumors. That's the great thing about small towns. News travels fast and often."

She laughed. "Yes. I finally convinced him I wasn't crazy, and we've been seeing each other. I'm...he's...it feels right, ya know."

"That's my girl. You were always stubborn, but your heart was in the right place. I'm glad to hear Grayson's realized there's no way to run from you." He laughed. "At least now I don't have to worry about what kind of trouble you'll get in trying to win his attention."

"About that…" She wrinkled her nose. "I'm sorry that I was such a hard kid to raise."

"Not hard. Interesting." He shrugged. "You were my daughter. I thought everything you did was cool."

"Cool, Dad?" She laughed. "Next thing you'll say is 'groovy.'"

"Don't blame me for trying to stay young," he said.

She threw her arms around his barrel chest and kissed his rough cheek. "I love you, Dad."

"Love you too, buddy." He took off his hat and swatted her backside. "Go on and get outta here. I need to get back to work."

She jogged to the car, and drove off. By the time she arrived at the lake and walked down to the water, Bruce already had a group of kids fishing in the pool and the adults stringing their poles. She checked in with the volunteers running the cash boxes, and later kept busy talking and catching up with old friends.

The hours flew by as she shuttled back and forth from the school to the lake to the park making sure everything ran smoothly. At five o'clock she called it another successful day.

Not having heard from Grayson all day, she hurried back to the hotel. While eating a peanut butter and jelly sandwich, she called Grayson's cell. After six rings, her call went to voice mail.

"Hey, it's me. Give me a call. I'm at the hotel." She paused. "Okay, call me soon. I missed you."

Not giving up, she called his house. When no one answered, she called the tennis center, and the desk personnel informed her Grayson had left hours ago.

She braced her elbows on her knees and stared at the floor. It was odd that she hadn't seen him all day. Not even a glimpse of him at the events.

Where are you, Grayson?

Chapter Twenty-Nine

"You're so full of shit, Schyler." Crista threw the throw pillow at Grayson's head. "Call Shauna and have her come over."

"No." He ducked. "The farther away she stays from me while the press is in town, the better. The benefit is almost over, and then I don't have to worry about someone questioning her. She's trying to make a name for herself and provide growth for Cottage Grove. I won't let anyone stop her from reaching her goal."

"Oh man, it's a good thing my sisters aren't here. They'd rip your balls off for taking the choice away from Shauna." Gary laughed.

"Hell, your sisters don't like any man. I think they'd use the occasion to throw a bashing party and take out the whole town." Grayson picked up the cushion and set it on his desk. "I can't believe you survived, growing up with six sisters. Not to mention every single one of them could stand in on any defensive line and win the damn game."

Gary nodded. "My momma raised us on meat and potatoes, what can you expect?"

"You should go talk with Shauna." Juan pulled his hair back in a ponytail and tied it with a rubber band. "She's worried."

"She's fine. Shauna is Shauna. She's throwing herself into raising money with everything she's got. Hanging around me will only distract her. She came back to Cottage Grove for one thing… to prove she was over bringing trouble down on her. When we're together, people will talk. The event is almost over, and then things will go back to normal." Grayson sighed. Was there such a thing as normal when Shauna was around?

"Still…if Shauna was my girlfriend, I wouldn't let her have any free time alone to think up ways to see me." Bruce stretched his arms over his head. "That girl has a wicked imagination."

"True. Trouble always follows her." Grayson burst out laughing. He rather liked not knowing what she was up to. It kept him on his toes. "You don't have room to talk. I don't see you guys calling your girlfriends."

"Women don't float my boat." Crista slapped Juan when he opened his mouth. "Shut up, Juan. Don't even talk."

"God, I love when you boss me around." Juan leaned closer. "We could be so good together."

Crista ignored him and gazed at Grayson. "I'm telling you… she doesn't deserve you."

"Enough. I'm through talking about Shauna." Grayson stood up. "If you were my friend, you'd see that this is the best thing I can do for her. You all know how hard the reporters work to drag up the past. Shauna's got more past than any of us. She doesn't need that kind of public humiliation right now. This is her moment."

Crista picked up her beer off the coffee table, drank, and continued to glare at him. "I've never understood how you could come to the conclusion that Shauna isn't smart enough to handle herself in any situation. When it comes to stupid males, you're right up there with the best of them. Any nice thing I've ever said to you in the past, I take back."

"I understand his pain." Dominic tossed a tennis ball in the air, caught it, and repeated the action again. "Women are awful. They never think about our feelings. They have no understanding that we hurt, and have pain too."

Crista swiped the ball before it could land in his hand. "Cry me a river, you big ox. I'm out of here. You guys can moan and whimper the rest of the night. I'm going for a run."

"You ran all day." Juan laid his good arm around her shoulder. "Why don't you and I take a stroll and—"

She elbowed him in the ribs. "Get lost, Juan, unless you want your other arm busted. I'm not one of your fan girls."

Crista left, the door slammed, and the following silence

irritated Grayson more than the lecture. He tossed the key ring to Dominic. He'd go to the house to find space to figure out how he could celebrate with Shauna after tomorrow's events. She deserved something big for all her hard work.

"Hey! Where are you going? I thought we were all staying a while at the center, opening the bottle of whiskey, and toasting our success." Juan sat down on the chair in Grayson's office. "We had a successful day."

"We could call Shauna and see if she wants to come over." Gary glanced at his watch. "It's not that late. What's her number? I'll call her."

"Leave her alone."

"Oh, come on. She wants to see you. I don't want her mad at me, thinking I didn't give you her message." Juan stifled a yawn. "She's worked harder than any of us, and deserves to relax and chill."

"Don't. Call. Her. I'm serious," he said.

"Grayson—"

"I'm outta here. Lock up when you're done and whatever you do, don't roughhouse and break up my office or ruin the courts." Grayson shut the door behind him.

Cottage Grove wasn't the place to hide from someone if you were looking for a place where no one would find you, especially Shauna. He hated resorting to old habits, but she had an event to oversee and he wouldn't do anything to embarrass her. He'd done that enough in the past.

He walked through the garage and out the back door into his private yard. With the others gone, he had the place to himself. He sat down at the edge of the pool, took his shoes and socks off, and stuck his feet in the water.

There had been a time when he used to sit out here in the dark. His parents were dead, Shauna was gone, and his manager would be asleep in one of the spare bedrooms, and he'd stare into the pool, imagining Shauna walking up to his front door after being away from him for years.

In his mind, he opened his arms and she ran toward him as if the time apart had meant nothing. He stared down into the water, watching the lights play off the surface. His career, the press, and his dreams never entered the equation. It was just him and Shauna, the way it was always supposed to be.

But she'd stayed in college, and he'd gone on to break records.

He gained a reputation as a charmer. He knew how to work the press. They called him the golden boy. Every time he played, he won, and he got more attention.

The only time he allowed himself to be the normal guy from Cottage Grove was around Shauna. He stood up. She'd forced him to remember, and accepted him with all his faults.

The phone rang in the house. He walked through the sliding door, and leaned over to read the caller ID. *Shauna.*

He reached out, snatched the phone off the counter, and pressed the button. "Shauna?"

"Hey, you." He could hear the contentment in her voice, and smiled. "I've been trying to get ahold of you all day."

He looked up at the ceiling. "Yeah, sorry. I've been busy. The center, the guys… How're the events going?"

"Oh, God. Better than I ever expected. The town is going crazy for the athletes and the money is rolling in." She laughed softly. "The biggest draw for the crowd happens tomorrow though. They can't wait to see you play. Me either."

"Good," he whispered, wanting to change the subject. "I miss you."

A lengthy silence came across the phone. "I could come over," she said.

He groaned. "Sweetheart, it's late. You're beat."

"Tomorrow night? When this is all over?"

He tapped his chest with his hand. "Definitely."

Shauna yawned. He chuckled. Nobody worked harder than her when she set her mind to doing something. She was wearing herself out.

"Go to bed," he whispered.

"'Kay."

He waited, but she remained on the line. "Shauna?"

"Okay, I'm going to sleep. Love you." She hung up the phone.

He held the phone in front of him, staring at the keypad. Her admission of love came freely and naturally. He smiled, tossed the phone onto the counter, and headed to his room, taking the stairs two at a time. Tomorrow night couldn't come soon enough.

Chapter Thirty

"He puts on a good show, doesn't he?" John stood beside Shauna, gazing through the window out to the court where Grayson hammed it up for the kids who challenged him for the first match.

"He's great with them. Even when I took lessons from him, he always kept the kids entertained and interested in tennis." She reached over and squeezed John's hand. "How have you been?"

"Good." He glanced at her. "I've been keeping busy with the dogs. I've survived having my heart broken…"

"John, I—"

"I'm kidding." He chuckled. "No, seriously. I'm fine. I never stood a chance with you, and I knew that. I do care about you, though. I'm happy you got what you wanted."

She turned and looked out at the man who meant everything to her. Warmth settled in her middle. Tonight, everything would be over and she'd be with Grayson.

"How's Blue?" she asked.

"I'm afraid he's not going to make the program." John scratched his chest. "He's more interested in gaining my attention than listening. I couldn't hand him over to a new family if I don't have confidence that he'll do his job."

"What will you do with him?"

"Rehome him. I don't have time or space for any more dogs that can't be trained for the handicap."

"Don't." She grabbed his arm. "I'll take him."

"Seriously?" John raised his brows. "Have you moved back in with your dad?"

She shook her head. "No, but I'm going to find a place to rent. I was going to get an apartment, but I'll rent a house that'll take pets...even if I have to move out of town farther to find cheaper rent. Can you hold on to him for a little longer?"

"Sure." He nodded. "I rather see him go to someone who'll love him, and I know you would."

"Thank you." She threw her arms around John. "You've made my day. I'm excited. I've never owned a pet before, but I'll learn everything there is to know."

He laughed. "I can help you. It's not hard."

A camera flashed. She ducked behind John.

"What's up with the pictures?" John looked over his shoulder.

"I don't know. They've been taking shots of me all day." She peeked around him. "Earlier they asked me if I was dating Grayson, and a whole bunch of nosy questions."

"What did you say?"

"The truth. I told them we're very happy and I've loved him forever," she said.

"Must be an article they're doing on the athletes. You might want to see if Grayson wants his private life broadcasted." John moved her out of the way as the crowd shifted. "Looks like the last match is over, and the Riddly boy won against Miller. That's good. He's been aiming for a chance to play Grayson one on one. He's damn good. I think he has a shot at going pro."

"That's my cue. Help me clear out the area around the press table. Grayson's promised the reporters a private interview before the final match." She dragged John along behind her.

Once everyone stood in front of the table, the press moved in and set up their cameras. Shauna looked at John and pursed her lips. The crew worked fast and efficiently, and she imagined they were used to battling the crowds to get a story, but she couldn't imagine having them trail her every day.

"Makes me glad I'm not famous." John chuckled.

"Me too," she whispered.

Mr. McMillian waved to her through the crowd and worked

his way over. "Shauna, you've pulled off a wonderful feat bringing Cottage Grove back to life. The amount of people at this event alone will make a difference."

"Thank you." She rubbed her arms. High praise coming from the man who hosted the biggest event of the year gave her goose bumps.

"My wife and I were talking, and once this is over, we'd love to have you help organize a fundraiser for the hospital that we're in charge of. It'll be nothing elaborate, only twenty or so of our friends at a sit down dinner. Your idea to bring celebrity athletes in to help draw the tourists to our small town was absolutely brilliant." He set his hand on her shoulder.

"Oh, well I couldn't have done it without Grayson. He—"

"Nonsense. Everyone is talking about it. From now on, when you call, people will come running." He winked.

"Thanks, I guess it won't hurt to talk with—"

"Wonderful!" He smiled. "I'll have Mrs. McMillian call you in a few days."

He left her with her mouth hanging open. What had just happened? Did the McMillians really want her help?

"Breathe." John laughed. "It wouldn't do any good if you passed out in front of everyone."

"I can't believe it. They want me?" She fanned her face with her hand. "Me? The wild child of Cottage Grove."

"Get used to it. You've made a name for yourself." John leaned over and kissed her cheek. "I can't stay. I need to get home and check on the dogs. This is your moment...congratulations."

She stood in a daze, and jumped when the microphone squelched. She turned toward Grayson, who stood behind the table, and smiled. He winked before turning his attention to the press.

"I'm ready to start." He nodded.

"Mr. Schyler, was today's event a sign that you're coming out of retirement and getting back in the game?" An older man scribbled on a notepad.

Grayson shook his head. "No. Cottage Grove is my home. I volunteered to participate in raising money to help boost the economy."

"Will you be playing in the Scottsdale tournament in Ireland in December?" A tall, pretty woman with red hair almost purred.

Shauna bit the inside of her cheek. She didn't like the way the woman was scoping Grayson out one bit.

"I will if you'll be there?" Grayson grinned.

"I'll make sure I am." She bowed her head.

Score one for the other team, Shauna fumed. She glanced at the clock. The hands stood still. How long did these things take?

"Speaking of dates. Who's your latest girlfriend?" The tall man she recognized from the other night at Grayson's leaned around her.

"I'm not answering personal questions. Please keep all questions sport related." Grayson gazed past her to the man hovering behind her.

She scooted over, but there were too many people blocking her way.

"Rumors are you've kept Shauna Marino tucked away, while you've paraded more than your fair share of beautiful women to the public." The man pressed against her back, not letting her escape. "Have you finally decided to show the world the real man off the courts?"

"You're excused from the interview." Grayson motioned Dominic and Gary to escort the man outside and away from the crowd.

Heat flooded Shauna's face, and she blinked rapidly to hide the pain of his denial. She understood his need to keep his private life private, but it still hurt.

"Brian Landow has asked you to come back and play against him. Do you have any plans to pick up the racket for your old rivalry? Maybe give him one more chance to beat the champion?" asked a man over on the left.

"No, but I've talked to Brian and invited him to come here to Cottage Grove and play me anytime he wants at my tennis center." Grayson winked. "He hasn't taken up the offer yet."

The crowd laughed. Shauna pulled the collar of her blouse away from her skin.

"Cal State confirms that you paid for Shauna Marino's tuition and sorority fees." The tall man shuffled closer to Shauna and continued. "Why would you risk your career for a woman who has done nothing but plague you continually while you were training? An under aged girl who you spent a lot of time with on and off the court? Did you pay for Shauna Marino's college education to keep her out of your life and to hide the scandal of having a relationship with a minor? Is she the reason you retired early?"

The room roared, and Shauna covered her mouth. She stared up at Grayson, and saw him set the microphone down on the table and walk out the door leading to the courts. Someone laid a hand on her arm, and she turned.

A flash went off, and she whirled around, pushing her way through the people. Dominic caught her hand, but she shook her head and pulled away. Was it really Grayson who'd sent her away from Cottage Grove?

Outside, she tried to gather her breath and focus on what happened. She paced the walkway in front of the center. How could he do that to her?

All this time, she'd thought her dad had scrimped and saved to give her an education when it was really Grayson who'd paid. She clenched her teeth together. How stupid could she be? Her dad struggled to break even his whole life. He couldn't afford to send her to Cal State.

She bunched her hands into fists. Grayson had played her. Not once had he forgiven her for all the past embarrassment she'd caused him. He'd waited, biding his time, until the moment was ripe to pay her back for all the trouble she'd caused him years ago. She'd fallen right into his hands by asking him to help with the benefit for the community. She'd brought the news crews, the reporters, to Cottage Grove, and he knew they'd investigate him. He didn't care, because for once, he could embarrass her in front of the town, just the way she'd done to him so many times in the past.

And he knew how much proving herself to the citizens meant to her. She'd confided everything, believing he was being honest. There was nothing scandalous about their friendship. He was her tennis coach. He was her friend.

Damn him.

He didn't even have the guts to stand there and face her, but left the meeting to direct all the attention toward her.

She turned and threw open the door. Everyone turned as she entered the lobby. She glanced through the window, assured that Grayson had started the match he'd promised as a finale to the fundraiser and lifted her chin.

She wasn't going to allow Grayson to shove her to the side and belittle their relationship. If the news crew wanted a story, she'd give them one. She'd already lost the respect she'd been striving for when she came back to Cottage Grove. Humiliating herself one more time to set the record straight wouldn't matter when all the evidence was damning enough.

"Ms. Marino, do you have a comment about the allegations that Grayson Schyler paid your way out of town after he'd run out of options to get rid of you? Can you contradict the statement and tell us the truth? Was there anything improper during your relationship when you were twelve years old and Grayson Schyler was a nineteen-year-old man? How about when you were sixteen and he was twenty-three and playing in his first Wimbledon tournament? Can you tell us when your relationship grew closer, when you became lovers?" The tall man thrust the microphone in her face.

She stared past him as other reporters were busy writing or fighting into position to hear what she said. Straightening her shoulders, she stared into the camera. She wanted to throw the ugly truth out for the world to see. To gain sympathy. To vindicate what Grayson had done to her. To scream out how much she was hurting.

The anger fizzled out of her. The quick temper and protective shell she'd surrounded herself in melted away, and a deep pain settled in her chest. She might never find love or someone who wanted her for who she was inside, but she wouldn't pay the price for the way others reacted.

Her mom's abandonment was not her responsibility.

Grayson's denial and lies were not in her control.

Her dad had lied.

She stared into the camera. "I've done a lot of things in the past that I'm ashamed of, but that is my burden and embarrassment to live with. I realize now that Grayson did not intend to include me in his life, and my feelings for him were not reciprocated. I had a teenage crush on a professional tennis player, nothing else. I wish Grayson well with achieving his dreams and his hopes for Schyler's Tennis Center. Cottage Grove is proud to be home to one of the world's finest men." She licked her lips. "I'd like to invite you all to stay and watch the finale match, but you'll have to excuse me. As the head of Cottage Grove's Chamber of Commerce, my job isn't over until the day is complete and I can announce the event a success."

Ignoring the stunned silence, she walked past the counter and out the front doors. Empty and in shock, she climbed into her car and drove away. Her life had fallen apart when her mom left, but not even that compared to learning the truth today. Not only did Grayson throw her love back in her face, he'd lied to her. Her dad had lied to her. She'd lied to herself.

Love does stop.

Chapter Thirty-One

Shauna's phone rang.

She scooped it off the top of her desk and tossed it in the bottom drawer. For good measure, she found her keys and turned the lock. She wasn't ready to talk with Grayson.

As far as she cared, everything was out in the open and nothing he could say would heal the hurt he'd caused. She had even left a message at the tennis center at two o'clock in the morning, two days ago, when he wouldn't be there to answer the phone, and asked him to please stop calling her. He only called more often.

She glanced at the clock, stood, and grabbed her purse. On the way out of the office, she waved to Ella without stopping to talk. If she hurried, she'd make it early to meet the girls and could make her excuses and leave before the crowd grew too big at the Quayside.

The curious stares and pitied looks she'd received only stung the wounds she already carried. In heels, she hurried along the sidewalk, gaze straight in front of her, arms swinging, pretending nothing was wrong. She could arrive at the lounge in five minutes, have a drink, and be home in less than an hour.

A motorcycle roared around the corner. She groaned and walked faster. *Please don't stop. Please don't stop.*

Grayson not only stopped, he hopped the curb and rode right onto the sidewalk and cut off her escape. She moved to the side. He rolled forward into her path.

She planted her fists on her hips. "Go away."

He removed his helmet at the same time he swung his leg off the bike. "We need to talk."

Sure, out here in public, where anyone could view the discussion and embarrass her more. She shook her head. That was so not happening.

"Shauna…" He reached for her and she stepped away. "Please. Let me explain."

"That's not necessary." She folded her arms, locking her purse against her chest. "I get it. You paid for my college, and even though you probably got to write it off as donating to charity, I will find some way to pay you back."

"Screw the money." His brows lowered. "It was a gift."

She snorted. No, it was a painful lesson. One she'd never repeat. He failed at asking her to stay away, because she was too stubborn to listen. He had been forced to pay her way out of town.

"Grayson, I'm going to be late. I have plans." She swung her arm out to the side. "Excuse me."

"We're not done." Grayson's hands dropped to his sides. "I miss you."

Her shoulders sagged before she caught herself. Lifting her chin, she gazed off to the side. "I need to go," she whispered.

"Okay, but we're not finished. You hear me?" he whispered back.

She swallowed hard and without answering, walked around his motorcycle and continued on her way to the Quayside. Willing herself not to look back, she counted her steps. One, two, three…

Ten minutes later, Shauna regretted her decision to meet the girls for a drink. Her friends were trying to be kind, but they were driving her crazy. She understood they were concerned about her and wanted to help, but there wasn't anything for them to do. She would recover and heal. In time, she might even be able to forget all about Grayson.

Coming to the Quayside was not a good idea, considering Grayson was on a personal mission to talk with her and she was doing her best to avoid him. She knew asking him to stay away wasn't enough. He'd ignored her wishes and as she sat down with Kate, Crista, and Diana, Grayson walked inside the restaurant as if he owned the place.

Everyone in the place seemed to know something big was going down.

Crista glared over Shauna's shoulder at the group of men who'd planted themselves on the other side of the lounge. A team, a force, they intimidated the whole town. That was the only reason the Quayside wasn't full of customers on a Friday night. The group of males held the power, but the females weren't out of options yet.

"I'll take out Juan. He'll be easy, cause he's under contract not to use his right arm." Crista leaned into the table, completing the circle of women. "Plus, I've always wanted to knock him down a peg or two."

Diana formed a fist. "Let me have the dumb Russian. He somehow found out my phone number and won't stop calling me."

"Dominic's calling *you*?" Crista's jaw dropped. "How? What?" Her mouth moved, but no sound came out.

"Settle down." Shauna patted Crista's arm. "I don't want you two fighting."

"Pshaw! She can have him. I've never met such an egotistical, uptight, little brained...*dick* in my life." Diana shuddered.

Kate caught Crista's arm and pulled her back down in the chair. "Okay, listen you two, we need to ban together. Solidarity and all that crap. We can do this. With Jackson on our side, it's five against five. I'm sorry, Shauna, but that leaves you to handle Grayson by yourself. Be strong. Be forceful. Be clever. If that doesn't work, knee 'im in the balls."

She groaned. "I love you all, but I'm fine. I'm going to walk out the door and let you all get back to enjoying the night. If I knew Grayson would come here and scare off all the customers, I would've gone straight to the hotel and skipped girls' night out. As it is, they'll probably never let me come back to the lounge. So much for my great idea to try and gain everyone's trust again."

"It's not right that he's following you around town," Diana said. "He's a bully."

"You've forgotten that this is how he's always been." She scooted her chair back. "I have a choice to react or rise above the situation. Since I spent my whole life reacting to everything he's done, I'm attacking this in a healthy, mature, and calm way."

Kate smiled. "I'm impressed."

"Thank you." She mustered a grin in return before turning to Crista. "I'm sorry about screwing up our last night together. I hope you'll come back to Cottage Grove and visit soon."

Crista stood up and leaned across the table to hug Shauna. "I will. I'll call you in a few days. I'll be in Hawaii training for the next three weeks, but we'll make plans."

Shauna stood up and hugged all of her friends, picked up her purse, and walked across the restaurant with her head held high. She tensed as she reached Grayson, Dominic, Bruce, Gary, and Juan, but to her relief none of them followed. She could only feel their stares heating up her backside as she walked past them out the front door.

Outside in her car, she couldn't help glancing in her rearview mirror, hoping Grayson would follow. By the time she arrived downtown and parked, she'd disgusted herself. No matter how hard she tried to move forward and concentrate on work, the truth was she wanted Grayson back. How sick was that?

He'd betrayed her in the worst way possible. Embarrassing her in front of the whole town, using his wealth and power to drive the wedge that should've killed the love she had for him, and what does she do? She inwardly allows him to continue hurting her.

What was it about her that caused people to want to run away? Her mom had thought nothing of leaving her own flesh and blood. Grayson hadn't even done that. Instead, he'd paid for her ticket out of Cottage Grove, convinced her dad to lie to her for all these years, and in the end, he'd left her unhappy and broken. Even her heart hurt.

I'll survive, I always do. She hoped she wasn't lying.

Ignoring the stairs that she usually took to her room at the hotel, she rode the elevator up to the third floor. Tomorrow, she'd contact Harvey Whittle at Keystone Realty and Properties and see about renting a home with a nice yard. Right now having Blue to cuddle would be the best medicine.

She hunted for her keycard in her purse, found it, and stopped when she looked up at her door. Her dad and mom flanked the wall, waiting for her. Great. Did they come to pour salt in her wounds or coddle her?

"Hi, buddy. How are you doing?" Tony swept off his cap and clutched it in front of him.

She glanced away from the worry in his eyes. "Exhausted. If you'll excuse me, I'm going inside and making it an early night. I'm bushed."

Her dad looked unconvinced and more than determined. He steeled his gaze and gave her *the look*, shrinking her to a ten-year-old. She had to remind herself that he'd let Grayson send her away and kept his secret. The one man she relied on to love her no matter how foolish she acted had betrayed her.

"Can we come in and talk with you? We won't stay long, I promise." Tony reached out and held Belinda's hand. "Please?"

She sighed and nodded, holding open the door and letting them enter her room. She pointed to the sofa for them to take a seat, set her purse on the table, and then perched on the remaining chair.

"I should've told you a long time ago, but Grayson asked me to keep it secret." Tony braced his elbows on his knees. "I'd love to tell you I honored his wishes because I wanted the best for you, and I knew I would never be able to afford to send you to college. But..."

She stared at the carpet, and remained silent. None of this meant much now, after the fact.

"The truth is I was ashamed. I was embarrassed. I'd already

failed as a husband, a father, and on a good day, I was happy if I managed to put food on the table and ask you how your day went." Tony ran his forearm across his eyes. "As your dad, I wanted to be the one to give you an education, a chance to broaden your dreams. I was tired of watching you beat yourself up every time someone in town made a comment about your crush on Grayson. I guess a small part of me also wanted him to pay, because I felt Grayson owed you. He hurt my little girl."

At some point in his speech, Shauna saw what he'd gone through being a single father. She had put him through hell, there was no denying it. All her days running wild and free after her mom left had given her time to find attention wherever she could find it. She'd forced Grayson into the position of accepting her, faults and all. She'd brought trouble upon herself.

"You did the best you could do, Dad. We both did." She moved over and kneeled beside him. "The more outlandishly I acted, I knew you'd stop whatever you were doing and come save me. It wasn't your fault. I don't blame you."

Tony hugged her. She squeezed her eyes closed, washing the moisture from them.

"I love you, buddy." He sniffed, and she managed to laugh when he ruffled her hair.

"I love you too."

"Shauna?" Belinda dabbed her cheek with Kleenex that she'd pulled out of her purse.

She moved back to the chair. "I don't mean to be rude, but there's really nothing that needs to be said between us. I've accepted that you're back in town and you're part of my dad's life, but I survived without a mother growing up, I certainly don't need one now."

"Shauna." Tony glanced over at Belinda. "Go on. Tell her."

"Dad, I—"

"No. You've forgiven me for letting Grayson pay for your

schooling, but what Belinda has to say is something else that I must take responsibility for." He leaned back. "Go on, honey. Tell her."

Nothing Belinda could say would change the fact that she'd left Shauna. She couldn't even look her mother in the face. Belinda was not the woman she remembered.

"I never wanted to be here, explaining what happened. To me, you're my daughter and there are certain things that no mother should tell her child." Belinda cleared her throat. "I forget that you're all grown up and have your own problems you're going through."

"This really isn't necessary," she said.

Belinda nodded. "You're right. I could walk out the door and forget about excusing my behavior, but I'm afraid everything I've done will continue to affect you. Each of us has our reasons why we act the way we do, and I can't tell you that I was wrong in leaving you, but I can tell you how sorry I am. I can't go back, and I'm not sure I would change how I handled the situation even if I could."

"Well, that's honesty." Shauna snorted. "Let's make both of us happy, and call it a night."

Belinda smiled, but her lips shook and the hand that she laid on her chest trembled. "You were always headstrong."

"Yeah, and that's what gets me in trouble," she muttered, as she picked at her thumbnail.

"I left you and Tony because he'd slept with another woman."

Her mother could've told her aliens had kidnapped her, and she would've given her the benefit of the doubt, but an affair? No way. Not her dad. He'd never even dated during the thirteen years after Belinda left.

"Are you really going to sit there and let her try to talk me into believing you cheated on her?" Shauna stared at her dad, waiting for him to tell his wife to stop.

He shook his head. "It's true. We were severely in debt after opening the body shop, and on the verge of bankruptcy. I'd gone out drinking and one thing led to another, and I cheated on your mom. I won't go into details, but your mom found out and confronted me. I told her the truth. I was already losing everything, and felt I didn't deserve her."

She blinked, absorbing the words but not understanding them. She wanted to scream, "What about me? What about your daughter? What about love?" Love wasn't supposed to stop because people make mistakes. Her chin dropped to her chest. Isn't that exactly what she let happen in her own life? Grayson had forgiven her for making his life difficult, and when she'd found out that he'd paid to send her away, she'd given up. *Oh God, I've been so stupid.*

She raised her head and glanced back and forth from her mom to her dad. They gazed back, waiting for her to say something. Their faces said it all. They wanted her to give them her forgiveness. They wanted to heal and move on as a family.

"You stayed away thirteen years," she whispered.

Belinda nodded. "I never planned on leaving you. I wanted to move away, get a job, an apartment, and come back for you."

"But you didn't."

"No." Belinda inhaled. "By the time I saved enough, I got sick and found out that I had cancer. Without insurance..."

Tony slipped her hand into his. "She didn't want to come back and burden me with medical bills, and take money away from raising you."

"It's okay, Tony. I can tell her." Belinda's voice came out stronger. "I obviously couldn't work and have treatments at the same time, and my boss, who was struggling with caring for his elderly mother who had Alzheimer's, suggested I move in with them and that way his mother would have a caregiver while he worked. He agreed to pay for my medical bills in exchange for the help I could give his mother. Before I had you, I was an RN, so I had the skills to help. Without money, I wouldn't have been able to afford treatment."

Shauna took the time to study her mom. That explained the added wrinkles and the frailness she saw lining Belinda's face. All the times she imagined her mother living it up, having no responsibilities, she'd really been fighting for her life and doing what she could not to take anything away from her daughter. She swallowed.

"The cancer?" She frowned.

"I'm in remission. It's been two years. It's come back three times in different parts of my body since the original diagnosis, but this is the longest I've gone cancer free." Belinda patted Tony's hand. "When my eighteen months scan came back clear, I called Tony and told him the whole story. I never stopped loving him, but I was scared. I didn't want to come back only to have you witness me dying. There will always be a risk that I'll develop more cancer, but I couldn't stand to be away from my husband and daughter any longer."

"But he cheated on you." Shauna rubbed her forehead. "How can you—"

"Loving someone can be a complicated situation. Humans make mistakes, and you can hate the situation, but still love the man." Belinda reached for Shauna. "Like you, I acted before thinking or talking it over. Your father's not to blame. We both are. I hope you can see through all our mistakes with you, and know that we love you. I want to know my daughter again. My beautiful and successful daughter that I thought about every single day I was gone."

A dam broke inside Shauna then and she flung herself into her mother's arms. She sobbed, pressing her face against her chest. She smelled painfully familiar, a pleasant mix of roses and fresh laundry hanging outside on a warm fall day.

Belinda held her close, while her dad reached over and stroked her hair. She closed her eyes and let the pain and hurt go.

Chapter Thirty-Two

"Shauna—"

She disconnected the call, powered down the cell phone, and shoved it in her back pocket. A small sigh escaped as she slid miserably onto the chair at the kitchen table. After politely asking Grayson not to call, show up at the hotel, send messages, and to stop sending her flowers, her only option to get him to halt his campaign to talk with her was to completely ignore him.

"Grayson again?" Tony passed her a bowl of chili.

A week had gone by after learning the truth of why her mom had left and as promised, she'd joined her parents for dinner. She was still going through with her plan to find somewhere to rent, but she was glad for the safety net of having her parents close by to help her.

She nodded. "I should change my phone number. Then Grayson won't be able to call me all the time."

Tony sat down beside Belinda and reached for the soda crackers. "Would that have worked with you?"

"What do you mean?" She stirred her food without taking a bite.

He raised his brows. "You were pretty determined to get his attention. Think about all the things you did. You can't fault a man for trying, especially after all the years he was more than lenient with you?"

"Touché." She groaned. "Maybe I should move away. I thought I could go through anything he put me through, and deal with all the talk from the town. I don't think I can anymore."

"No." Belinda reached across the table and caressed Shauna's arm. "Don't run. You'll regret it for the rest of your life."

"It hurts. How can I be furious with Grayson, and still love him?" She laid her hands in her lap, wanting to curl up in a ball and forget about everything. "Listen to me. I even sound crazy to myself. Maybe I need a therapist."

Tony stepped behind her and wrapped his arms around her. "That's love, buddy. Those who love us have the ability to hurt us the most, but you have to allow yourself to be vulnerable. That's the only way you'll experience love."

She patted her dad's arm before standing up. "I'm going to walk back to the hotel. I have paperwork I need to go over. A developer contacted the building code department about the bare land out on Seventy-Eighth Street. They're interested in building a strip mall."

"No kidding?" Tony chuckled. "Won't that be something?"

"Eat first." Belinda pointed to the table. "You need to keep up your energy with all the work you do."

"I'm okay." She smiled. "I'll grab something at the hotel if I get hungry."

She kissed both of them, and walked out of the house. The two-mile stroll back to town would clear her head. She'd had a hard enough time concentrating lately, and maybe her mom was right. She had to put closure to her old dreams and focus on moving forward.

At the end of the block, Jerry Tonk turned around from washing his car. She stopped at the edge of his driveway. "How are you, Mr. Tonk?"

"It's a good day. My arthritis won't kill me. At least that's what Doc Martin says." He tossed the sudsy mitt in the bucket. "Stop by and share some cookies with me soon."

"I'd love that," she said.

"Bring your young man, Grayson, with you too." Jerry sprayed the suds off the fender.

She waved, and continued on her way. There was no use

explaining that there was no Grayson in her life. No one ever believed her.

At the end of the street, she turned left. She stared straight ahead, but she could still see the tennis center out of her peripheral vision. When she'd set out to walk to her parents' house, she knew she was putting herself in a direct path of catching a glimpse of Grayson. She would excuse her behavior as an old habit, but she'd be lying.

There were a couple of ways she could remedy the situation. One was to pack a suitcase, hop on the soonest flight, and send herself clear across the world. She could move into a little chateau, somewhere that had no phone service and no one spoke English. The other choice would be to listen to what he had to say. She was tough. What was the worst that could happen?

She picked up her pace. *I should really consider moving.*

When was the last time she'd walked through town, along her old route, and past the school? She knew this road by heart. Had kicked rocks, sold lemonade, and crashed on her bike more times than she could count.

Yet today her walk felt different. The houses a little more weather worn, the trees taller, and the asphalt dotted with potholes. She slowed down, and put her hands in her pockets. It wasn't her surroundings that'd changed. It was her.

She'd always had a purpose before. This road took her to the tennis center, and Grayson was always her reward at the end of the day. Every morning on the way to school, she'd wave to Grayson as he walked from his house to his lessons. On the weekends, she'd hang out, pretending to walk to town in the chance that Grayson was outside, and then she'd make an excuse to talk with him.

What did she have at the end of the road today? She sighed. An empty hotel room and a load of truth that was too heavy to carry.

A car pulled out of the school parking lot. Shauna stopped and smiled at Mrs. Winlet, the principal, as she drove by. Now that was one woman she remembered well. She'd spent many hours in her office, convincing her to give her one more chance. She gazed over at the high school. Oh, lordy.

Across the top of the roof, in faded red paint, were the words "Grayson's #1." She brushed a tear from her cheek. He was supposed to have been impressed with her creativity and climbing skills.

It'd taken her over an hour, in the pre-dawn hours, to carry her dad's extendable ladder through the neighborhood without being caught. Not to mention, she was afraid of heights. It wasn't so bad climbing up, but working up the nerve to hang off the gutter to find the ladder had been too much. Mr. Krieger, the janitor, had had to come and help her down. She'd instantly vomited the Snickers bar she'd snuck for breakfast, in front of the kids arriving at school.

She continued walking. One thing had stood out that day. Grayson.

He'd stared out from his manager's car as he'd driven past the school. She would've missed his reaction, but at the last second, his gaze had swung from the roof to the side of the equipment shed before he rounded the corner out of sight. In that microsecond, they'd connected and he'd smiled.

It wasn't a full-toothed grin, but more a slight curve of his lips. Her stomach fluttered, remembering. It had been enough to make the weeklong detention and community service punishment worth it.

Two young girls whizzed down the road on each side of Shauna. She glanced behind her as they passed.

"That's her!" The blond-haired girl laughed.

The other girl stopped and turned to meet Shauna's gaze. "Hey, lady? Is it true you're the one who wrote on the bottom of the screen at the movie theater?"

"The Kiggins Theater in town?"

The girl giggled. "Yeah, that one. It says, 'SM loves G.'"

That one hadn't been her idea. Kate had promised she'd write on the screen if Shauna did it first. She hadn't even finished Grayson's initials before one of the workers caught her.

"That was me. I wouldn't advise doing anything like that though. I got in a huge amount of trouble, and my dad made me apologize during the Harvest parade." Shauna raised her brows. "Totally embarrassing."

"I think it's cool." The other girl got back on her bike. "Who's G?"

"Who?"

"G. The person you loved?"

Shauna shrugged. "Just a boy."

Without any more details coming from Shauna, the girls rode away, and Shauna took off in the opposite direction. She walked faster and swung her arms. Walking down memory lane wasn't helping her situation.

She couldn't make all her mistakes go away. The best she could hope for was making the town satisfied with the job she'd done raising money for the community.

Grayson was a part of her life, whether he wanted to be included or not. It didn't take a bronze statue in the middle of the park to show everyone's respect and admiration. She'd created a town full of memories.

Chapter Thirty-Three

It was late when Grayson left the center. He walked the driveway to a lonely house. More than ever before, he hated the silence. He missed having Shauna's laughter filling the room, and her warm body curled around him in bed. The silence ate away at his mental stability.

He moved forward on autopilot. The grim reality that life would be empty and meaningless without Shauna depressed him. He had no one to blame but himself.

Every time he'd tried to tell her why he'd sent her away to college, she'd refused to listen. Hell, his excuses sounded even stupid to him. She had a right to be mad. He'd taken the decision out of her hands, because he was selfish.

He was out of ideas on how to make their relationship right. For once, he'd give anything to have her imagination. Never before had he felt so utterly useless.

He drew in a deep breath and opened his front door. His head ached. Not willing to give up yet, he plopped down on the couch and punched in her number on the phone. He scowled as he waited.

"Hello?" Shauna's soft, sultry voice echoed in his head.

"Please, don't hang up."

"Okay."

He blew out his breath. "How are you?"

"Good."

He shook his head. Stupid question. "Shauna, I wanted to…"

Silence sent his heart to pounding. He didn't want to do this over the phone. He wanted to see her, touch her, and make her understand all the emotions overwhelming him. She had to know that she'd done nothing wrong, and that it wasn't her fault they were both miserable.

"I'm sorry," he said.

"I know," she whispered. "I'm sorry too."

"No, it's my fault." He cleared his throat. "I blew up when the reporters pressured me and everything got out of hand before I could gain control of the situation. I didn't want you hurt. I never wanted you to find out I paid for your education this way."

"I guess we're even."

"This wasn't a game, Shauna. It was never about paying you back." He leaned forward and braced his elbows on his knees, holding the phone to his ear. "I can't do this over the phone. Will you come over or let me come to you?"

Seconds ticked by. He closed his eyes, whether to protect him from the answer or wishing for her to agree, he had no idea.

"I'm sorry. I can't." Her gulp had him cradling his forehead in his hand. "I've thought a lot about us, Grayson, and I'm confused. I need to clear my mind, and figure out what I'm going to do next...on my own. I think it's time I learn about myself and improve my life, and I'm not sure I can do that around you."

"I'm not giving up on us."

"Maybe it's time," she said. "Maybe I've hung on to you for too long."

"Don't say that." Grayson stood up, ready to beg her to listen to him, but she'd hung up.

He held the phone in front of him, staring at the buttons.

His heart ached, and he felt physically broken, hearing the defeat in her voice. Would she ever come back to him?

The reality of what he'd done dropped him to his knees. The throbbing started in his stubborn head and pierced his chest. He'd closed himself off from loving anyone after his parents abandoned him for a childfree lifestyle. He'd concentrated on moving up in the ranks to become the world's best tennis player, and for what?

What did he have to show for all those years of keeping to himself and never allowing himself to love?

Shauna had changed him. She had helped him retain normalcy in a world that seemed unusually harsh and cold. He'd been wrong to push her away and deny love between them because he was afraid.

He rolled over onto his back and stared up at the ceiling. She had no idea how much he loved her. He'd make sure she never doubted him ever again.

He'd start tomorrow, and wouldn't give up until he'd convinced her to let him love her for the rest of his life.

After a restless night, morning came early. Grayson tidied the mess around the house, and was out the door by nine o'clock. It was imperative that he arrive at the newspaper office before the newspaper hit the printing press for the day.

He didn't care how much it cost him, but if Shauna could play dirty…so could he. Roses and chocolates weren't the way to her heart. He should've known better. If anyone was simple in a complex way, it was Shauna.

She did everything big, without a thought to how she looked to others. That was what he loved about her. She went with her feelings, and ignored the naysayers. He'd show her that he was worthy of her love.

Twenty minutes later, he walked out of the *Daily News* office. He couldn't keep the smile off his face. Mr. Gunderson had even clapped him on the back and given him encouragement when he'd explained his dilemma.

He walked down to the corner, turned, and jogged the two blocks to the city road department. If Shauna wanted proof of how much he loved her, he'd make sure she and everyone in Cottage Grove had no doubts.

By the time he was through, he had more energy than if he'd reentered the pro circuit and came off the court winning. He dialed his cell as he walked.

"John?" He lowered his voice. "It's Grayson. Can I come out to your place? I have a business proposition for you."

When he hung up, he grabbed the first person he saw. Mrs. Lubitz gasped when he kissed her full on the lips.

"What in the world has gotten into you, Grayson?" Mrs. Lubitz pressed her hand on her chest. "I'm eighty-seven years old. Are you trying to give me a heart attack?"

"No, ma'am." He grinned. "Have a nice day."

He laughed as she stood in the middle of the sidewalk, staring after him. Wanting to share his happiness, he put the top down on his car, cranked the stereo, and headed out of town.

When he arrived at John's house, it took him an hour to convince Shauna's friend that his intentions were honorable. Grayson stood in the driveway and clapped John on the shoulder. "Thank you. This means the world to me."

"I'm not doing this for you. Shauna deserves all the happiness she can find, but I'm not sure you're the man who can make that happen." John squinted. "You have no idea how much I'd love to kick your ass for how much you've hurt her. I also don't think I'm the only one in town who thinks that way."

"I'll agree with you there." Grayson sighed. "People in this town haven't said two words to me lately."

John raised his brow. "Shauna's a special friend to me. I hope you know what you're doing."

"I don't have a clue." Grayson shoved his hands deep in the front pockets of his jeans. "I only know that I'll do anything to have her back, and I won't stop until she understands how much I love her."

John studied him for a few seconds and finally, shaking his head, walked off. "Good luck, man. You're gonna need it."

He had no doubt about that. He had nothing to lose, and everything to gain. The last week had given him a lot of time to think about why he'd refused to discuss Shauna to the press, why he'd sent her away, why he'd retired at the prime of his career, and why he'd continued to hurt her every time she tried so damn hard to show him how much she loved him. The charges against him were damning, but his heart told him not to give up.

He was falling apart. He needed Shauna in his life.

All the money and fame in the world meant nothing if he lost her in the process. He had to be strong enough to ask for her back, and have enough faith in himself to trust that it would work. For the first time, something mattered more than protecting himself. He could say the words he'd longed to tell her since he'd sent her away. She'd opened his eyes, and never again did he want to be the cause of all the pain he saw in hers.

Chapter Thirty-Four

Shauna held her hand to her stomach and wished the nausea away. It was bad enough that she had dark circles under her eyes. She didn't want to embarrass herself further by throwing up in the middle of the town meeting.

A knock, followed by Ella sticking her head into the office and giving her a thumb up, almost sent her to hyperventilating. She'd grown closer to the members of the city council during the time since she began working on the benefit. She'd gained the town's respect, and the last thing she wanted to do was bring up the dastardly way the fundraiser had ended back to the forefront of everyone's mind.

She picked up the box full of files and followed Ella down the hall. Everyone sat, waiting and depending on her. A knot tightened in the pit of her stomach. Afraid? Yes.

She'd wanted their acceptance her whole life. She owed the whole town. She'd been a wild child, a troublemaker, but she'd meant well.

She'd distanced herself in the past whenever anything went wrong, and lately the looks cast her way were not of pity, but of concern and love. She could see that now. She'd allowed them to think the comments didn't hurt, but she couldn't blame them for laughing. The antics she'd created in her past were those of a child desperately looking for love. After all these years, she was still looking for love.

A funny thing about small town living was you never outran your mistakes. She was okay with that. The way her mom and dad had moved past their troubles and found each other again proved to her that love never went away, no matter how hard you try to run.

"The accountant finished all the paperwork and I hope you'll be pleased with the success we had with our first fundraiser." She passed out the folders. "The local businesses have also included the added revenue the flood of tourists brought to Cottage Grove during their visit to our city."

"What about the…um, vandalism done at the hotel?" Dan peered down his nose at the papers.

She smiled. Dominic's fans had broken the locks on two of the doors at the hotel after rumors that the hockey player might be staying there. Luckily, Dominic had been hiding at Grayson's house under tight security and the rooms at the hotel had been vacant at the time.

"The repairs were paid for by Mr. Chekovsky himself." Shauna sat down and waited.

Mrs. Bakkersten whistled. "Are you sure this figure is right?"

Shauna nodded. "It's a rough estimate on the low side but yes, there were at least fifteen thousand tourists visiting Cottage Grove over the three-day event."

"My God," Mr. Stephenson whispered. "The events alone raised over three hundred thousand dollars."

"Mr. Winston brought in over thirty-two thousand dollars above his normal profit, mainly in selling batteries, snacks, and drinks," Ella said, winking at Shauna. "Each business along Grayson Schyler Street has their own victory story they've shared in the rest of the documents."

Mrs. Bakkersten shook her head in amazement, gazing over at Shauna. "You've singlehandedly boosted the economy of the town, young lady."

"Well, not yet, but we're heading that way. I've already started on planning next year's event. Crista Johnson has been kind enough to get me in contact with the country singer Jude Lovelaw, and between him and the Flying Blues putting on an airshow, I think we can count on another successful fundraiser. That's if every one of us is in agreement?" She held her breath.

"Hell yes! I mean, heck yes." Mrs. Bakkersten blushed. "This is the best news I've heard in my thirty years of being on the city council. We can't thank you enough, Shauna."

She smiled. "No thanks necessary. This is my town too."

Dan cleared his throat and stood up. "I have to admit, I was worried after what happened at the tennis center during the press conference."

And there it was. The one thing she hoped everyone would've ignored. She crossed her legs under the table and met their gaze. "Yes, about that. I can guarantee that won't happen again."

"I hope that's not true." Dan frowned. "After reading the write up in the paper this morning, my wife and I agreed that it was the best thing that's ever happened in Cottage Grove. You and Grayson have both been a huge part of this town your whole life. We've all rooted for you your whole life that you'd catch our Grayson. We're all ecstatic that you finally won."

She glanced around at everyone. They sat smiling and nodding at her. "What article?"

"You didn't read the paper, dear?" Mrs. Bakkersten pointed at Dan and motioned toward the door. "Go get her the newspaper on my desk."

Dan quickly returned and plopped the front page on the table in front of her. She bent over and started reading.

In a bold move made by the newly hired head of Cottage Grove's Chamber of Commerce, Shauna Marino has succeeded where others have failed. In a once shriveling small town, Shauna Marino's return to take over the Chamber of Commerce has breathed life into Cottage Grove's business sector, the citizens, and the town's golden boy, Grayson Schyler, with pure determination, love, and dedication.

She skimmed the next four paragraphs explaining what went on during the three days of events, and started reading the last paragraph.

In an emergency press conference on September thirtieth, Grayson Schyler met with reporters outside the Grayson Schyler Tennis Center. With much more fanfare than he showed during his announcement to retire from the sport of tennis, Mr. Schyler announced to everyone present that he was going on record to say that he loved Ms. Marino, and he would not rest until she agrees to be his wife. When asked about his future, and any chance of returning to the court, he smiled and was quoted as saying, "No. My next plan after Shauna agrees to marry me is to convince her to have my babies."

A teardrop fell on the bottom of the paper. She lifted her gaze in wonder. "He loves me?"

Mrs. Bakkersten walked around the table and put her arm under Shauna's elbow, lifting her to her feet. "Of course he does, dear. We've all known he's loved you, he just fought too hard not to show it."

"You knew?" She let Mrs. Bakkersten lead her toward the door.

"Absolutely. We all saw how much he loved you, and you loved him. Even back when you were young and chasing that man like a damn fool, we never gave up hoping that you'd get him." Mrs. Bakkersten gave her a quick hug and turned her around with a little push. "Now go outside. I know for certain that there's someone waiting to talk to you, and you know how impatient he can be. You better not keep him waiting."

Her thoughts floated around her as she made her way to the front of the building and stepped out the door. She scanned the area, but didn't see anyone. Confused, happy, and a little scared, she wandered out to the sidewalk.

She gasped. *Grayson!*

There he was, leaning against her car, rubbing the back of his neck, staring at the ground. She walked toward him slowly. His hair was a mess, his shirt wrinkled, and he kept scuffing the toe of his sneaker against the curb. Her heart filled with warmth. He looked miserable.

She sped up, and looped into a jog. Tears rolled down her face, and when he lifted his head and spotted her, she sobbed. He stepped up on the sidewalk and opened his arms. Without hesitating, she flew into his embrace.

"I'm sorry," he murmured, running his hands through her hair and kissing her face. "I've been an asshole. I never meant to hurt you. I love you."

She hiccupped. "I love you too. I always have, and I'll never stop."

"When you wouldn't call me back or open your door, I thought I'd lost you." He pulled back and cupped her cheeks, making her look at him. "You've asked me why I retired while in the prime of my career, and it's because tennis never gave me the one thing I desired more than anything. Love. You gave me that, sweetheart. I want to marry you."

"Oh, Grayson." She kissed him.

A crowd gathered across the street and clapped. She broke the kiss and buried her head in the crook of his neck, laughing. Somewhere in the distance, a dog barked and she was vaguely aware of people cheering.

"Please say that's a yes," he groaned.

She lifted her head. "Of course it's a yes. Yes! Yes! Yes!"

He swept her off her feet and twirled her around, holding her to his chest. She laughed and cried happy tears.

"There's something I have to show you." He set her back on the ground, and took her hand.

She gazed up at him, smiling. "I keep thinking I'm dreaming. You've made me so happy."

He leaned over and gave her a kiss. "I love you."

A dog yapped, and she turned her head. Ahead of her, tied to a street sign, Blue jumped, trying to break free and run to her. "It's Blue! What's he doing here?"

"I asked John to let me have him. He needs a home, and I have the perfect backyard." He undid the knot and handed the leash to Shauna.

"Thank you." She kneeled down and petted Blue. "How about that, Blue? A family, a new home, and lots of love all in one day."

"There's one more surprise." Grayson smiled and pointed up in the air.

She tilted her head, read the street sign, and burst out laughing. "You're crazy."

"I'm crazy for you." Grayson wrapped his arm around her. "You forgot that you promised to name another street after me if I helped you with the benefit. Seeing as how I already had one I thought you should have one yourself."

"That's crazy, Grayson." She smiled. "And I love it."

He scooped her up in his arms and whispered, "Our home is here in Cottage Grove, where Grayson Schyler Street meets Shauna Marino Avenue."

About the Author

Top Selling Romance Author Debra Kayn lives with her family in the beautiful coastal mountains of Oregon on a hobby farm. She enjoys riding motorcycles, gardening, playing tennis, and fishing. A huge animal lover, she always has a dog under her desk when she writes and chickens standing at the front door looking for a treat. She's famous in her family for teaching a 270 lb. hog named Harley to jog with her every morning.

Her love of family ties and laughter makes her a natural to write heartwarming contemporary stories to the delight of her readers. Oh, let's cut to the chase. She loves to write about *REAL MEN* and the *WOMEN* who love them.

When Debra was nineteen years old, a man kissed her without introducing himself. When they finally came up for air, the first words out of his mouth were… "Will you have my babies?" Considering Debra's weakness for a sexy, badass man who is strong enough to survive her attitude, she said yes. A quick wedding at the House of Amour and four babies later, she's living her own romance book.

You can visit Debra's website at *www.debrakayn.com*
Follow her on Twitter at *www.twitter.com/DebraKayn*
Like her Facebook Page at *www.facebook.com/DebraKaynFanPage*

In the mood for more Crimson Romance? Check out *Taming the Stallion* by Dorothy Callahan at *CrimsonRomance.com*.